The Trials of Sherlock Holmes

by

James Moffett

Paperback ISBN 978-1-78705-135-5
ePub ISBN 978-1-78705-136-2
PDF ISBN 978-1-78705-137-9

Published in the UK by MX Publishing
335 Princess Park Manor, Royal Drive,
London, N11 3GX
www.mxpublishing.co.uk

Cover design by Brian Belanger

To Mum and Dad for their love and constant support.

Contents

Preface

Due to the deep repercussions and sensitive nature of the Bloomsbury Scandal, which reached its height in the month of December 1888, the reasons for which will soon become clear, I felt it necessary to allow a number of years to pass before the public could be informed of the events that led up to its resolution. Meanwhile, this gave me the opportunity to publish some other less-delicate accounts from my adventures with Mr Sherlock Holmes.

With the scandal now long-buried in the annals of history, it seems an appropriate time to bring these events back to light. I have therefore endeavoured to collate a selection of stories from our cases which relate exclusively to this incident, and have taken the liberty of collecting these writings under the present title.

John H. Watson, M.D.
1895

The Hanging Man

The year 1887 was an exceptional one for crime. The Knightsbridge Horror, the Edgware Robbery, the Mayfair Crisis – to mention but a few of the most notorious that made the headlines and caused sensational gossip. Not that London was ever purged from the incessant stream of violence and decadence that human insensibility was capable of. Yet, wherever crime flared, my friend Sherlock Holmes was always there to douse the flames and bring matters to order. His methodical reasoning and sharp analytical skills were sought by many: from the noblest of clients to the poorest of victims. Of the lost souls from Scotland Yard, who pounced on every opportunity to seek his advice and counsel, much is told elsewhere. His hunting grounds were this great city's endless streets and hidden alleyways. He was the bane of schemers and murderers, and the hero of victims; elements of human nature were unimportant to Sherlock Holmes. He was like a machine, unvarying and unflinching to emotions, destined only to race on for the rest of its life, unchanging and interminable.

It was on an early November morning that I found myself having breakfast at our lodgings at 221B Baker Street. Whilst a clattering noise rose up from downstairs, as Mrs Hudson busied herself with the daily housekeeping, I ate in silence, wondering at the whereabouts of my friend. It was a particularly chilly morning and having no patients to attend to that day I indulged myself by rising well after the sun was up. It was now a quarter past ten and my companion would, had he been present, already be sitting in his armchair by the fire going through the daily newspapers, hoping to gather any scrap of information to liven his boredom. Or else he would be hunched over his laboratory equipment as he tested carbonated compounds and sulphuric acids. I was aware that there had been no significant cases for over a month and, following the rather speedy clearing up of the Rolestine family affair just over a week ago, Sherlock Holmes had been even less communicative than was his norm.

As I pondered on these matters at the kitchen table, I heard the soft and unmistakable sound of footsteps ascending the stairs. Our landlady walked in as I had just finished my breakfast.

"A telegram for you Dr Watson," said Mrs Hudson, as she handed over the slip of folded paper and went back down to her chores. Making my way to the sitting-room, closer to the windows overlooking Baker Street, I opened the telegram.

New case in hand.
Find me at 19, Weighhouse Street
– S.H.

I could not help but smile at the words. Clearly, my friend had found a new opportunity to demonstrate his skills and alleviate the tediousness for the coming day or two. His brief note reminded me of the machine's gears locking into place and gathering speed: a train that would stop at nothing until the mystery was solved and any culprits brought to light. Snatching up a woollen scarf along with my coat and top hat, I descended the stairs. The sun had risen above the smoking chimneys of Baker Street, but the keen bite of cold air greeted me as I headed outside. Calling a hansom and directing the driver to the address given by my friend, we headed towards Weighhouse Street and soon disappeared among the busy commuters populating the city's thoroughfares.

My destination lay only twenty minutes from 221B and the street itself was more of a short road running parallel to Oxford Street. As the cab ground to a halt at the intersection between Duke Street and Brown Hart Gardens, I tucked the scarf closer to my neck. The narrow alleyways funnelled most of the cold north-westerly air and dispersed it among the labyrinthine architecture of this part of London.

Weighhouse Street was lined on either side with red brick houses and at this time of day the sun had yet to cast its warm rays on the shadowed path before me. I found myself walking down that rather peaceful passage as the rumble of bustling life could be heard in the distance. It was a respectable area by all accounts and as I observed the numbers on the varnished, black wooden doors, I found no difficulty in identifying the specific house where I was expected. Whereas the neighbouring houses had a quaint appearance with bright clean windows and well-tended fence railings, no. 19 was Weighhouse Street's exposed scar: it stood out from the rest by its shabby look, grinning in mockery at the rest of the buildings and any passersby. As I approached the house, out of its unwholesome façade emerged two police officers whose stumbling walk and pale faces made me wonder what possible grim discovery they had just witnessed, and where might my friend be found inside.

Uncertain in my gait, I hesitantly peered through the half-opened door and cautiously stepped inside. I found myself in a long dark corridor that faded towards blackness, a soft light emerging from the first room on the left. In that faint light, I discerned what remained of the dark green wallpaper peeling off the walls of the corridor. A large gash was visible just above the skirting close by the door. The elaborate design on the carpet under my feet, that had once undoubtedly been a welcoming sight, was faded and worn. As I took a step forward, out of the side room emerged a short, hunched figure in a long dark dustcoat. His face was instantly familiar. I had been first introduced to that man during our adventure in *A Study in Scarlet*. By all accounts, Inspector Lestrade was not the brightest of individuals, but his familiar presence in that house lifted my spirits.

"Dr Watson," he uttered quietly as he recognised me and beckoned me forward. There was something in the tone of his voice that made me uneasy and warned me against the contents within the lit room he was directing me to. Even the Scotland Yard detective, familiar with the brutal London underworld, had been shaken by something unusual. Although accustomed to the sight of violence and wounds inflicted during wars, I myself was taken aback by the sight that greeted me.

The room was small, with a wooden cabinet filled with books at the far end of the left wall and a grimy fireplace with roaring flames on the other side. The fire had an eerily green hue to it that transformed the atmosphere of the room into an even more unsettling one. In the centre was a desk littered with papers and writing implements.

Then my eyes fell on the awful scene for which I had been called. My sight had yet to adjust to the strong bright light that shone through the two windows at the far end of the room on either side of the desk. The curtains had been pushed aside and in front of the left window there appeared the silhouette of a man, standing stiff with his head to one side. To my astonishment, he seemed to be floating in the air, until I noticed a thick line extending from around his neck and reaching up to the ceiling. Closer inspection showed that the face had been covered by some sort of theatrical mask with wrinkled skin and a grotesquely elongated nose. This prop disturbed me more than anything else. What twisted mind could have conjured up such an act? A chill ran down my spine. I felt cold and a strong sweet smell pervading the room made me feel slightly nauseated.

Before I had time to recover from this ghastly scene, I noticed a second figure sitting down at the desk with its back towards me. The upper body was lying flat on the surface of the desk and the face was concealed from my view. As I stood there at the entrance, Lestrade pushed past me and I grudgingly took another step forward, with the wooden floor creaking beneath my right shoe.

"Brick dust!" exclaimed a voice.

I was certain it had not been Lestrade who, together with myself, was the only living individual in that accursed room.

"Distinctive pattern formations," it repeated.

I staggered back into the corridor as I saw the second body move and rise out of the chair. It turned round to face me and, just before I found myself fleeing from the house, I recognised the features of my friend on the figure who was now standing upright and holding a small magnifying glass in his right hand.

"Watson! Delighted you could join me in this little riddle of mine."

Sherlock Holmes had the remarkable ability of ignoring most human emotions being displayed right in front of him. While he could describe the character of an individual from his clothing or the state of his kitchen, he could be completely oblivious towards the obvious and the normal. I was still reeling from the shock in thinking I had been witness to a supernatural occurrence. I stepped back into the room somewhat vexed by my companion's antics. Inspector Lestrade had been silent during the whole performance, whilst keeping a close look on the wretched individual hanging from the ceiling.

"What on earth were you doing, Holmes? I thought you were just another body in this awful house," I declared, as my nerves began to calm down at the collected composure of my friend.

"Some would agree with you, that my inability to act like any other human being renders me just so," he replied. Having put the magnifying glass inside one of his waistcoat pockets, Sherlock Holmes clasped his hands behind his back and began pacing the room.

"Lestrade called me early this morning after an anonymous note was sent to Scotland Yard with directions to this house," he said.

"Mr Holmes, I called you in on this case since I knew you took an interest in these fantastical tricks," sighed Lestrade as he gestured at the mask, "but I think what happened here is simple enough."

"On the contrary. It is simplicity itself that makes this case so delightfully complex and fascinating."

"How so?" I inquired, feeling the initial horror of the scene slowly fade away as I became more intrigued by Holmes and his usual routine of conducting a critical analysis of a case. He gave a small chuckle and walked towards the hanging man.

"Watson, what details can you point out upon observing your surroundings?"

I smiled, knowing that whatever was plain in sight for me to see was nothing compared to what Sherlock Holmes had already examined and rationally processed in his mind. Nevertheless, the thrill of attempting some of my friend's methods was too tempting not to try.

However, looking round, I could discern little else apart from the obvious. The room was small and acted like some sort of office. The piles of books in the cabinet and the papers littering the desk were good indications that the owner was a man of trade. A small wooden box, presumably belonging to the victim, had been placed next to the papers and had a neat inscription on its lid:

A. V. Gordon
Horrigan Industries Ltd.

As far as I could recall from the newspapers, Horrigan Industries was owned by a wealthy family engaged in the coal-mining business. Clearly, this was a man employed in the services of the Horrigans in a high-ranking position, given his surroundings and attire which, although weathered and unkempt, spoke of a once well-off individual. I described all these observations and thoughts to my friend who had sat down again on the chair. He had closed his eyes and rested his elbows on the desk with his fingertips touching together. I could see the intensity with which he took in every word I spoke by the twitching of his eyebrows. I concluded my remarks by stating the rather solid possibility that the man had found himself in financial difficulties and, in desperation, had taken his own life. The chipped edge of the desk appeared to mark the spot on which he had climbed in order to attach the rope to one of the unsteady roof beams and step to his death.

"Suicide, clearly," interjected Lestrade, agreeing with my conclusion. The signs were all there. The mask placed on the man's face could have been a last laugh at life itself or a final salute to his creditors who would now be unable to make up their losses. I looked back at Holmes who, upon realising I had finished my analysis, sprang out of the chair and once again began pacing round the room with agility and excitement. The machine was working itself into gear.

"Excellent analysis!" said Holmes. "Now that our good Inspector and Dr Watson have eliminated every possible inaccuracy, we can move on to the real facts." I sighed as I realised this was Holmes' usual way of demonstrating the potential of an uncompromising mind set upon solving a mystery.

"The first mistake is to assume that what lies before you is the truth. Someone enters a room and sees a man hanging from a ceiling. They immediately come to the conclusion that he has killed himself. The state of this house, perhaps, might indicate a disregard for life itself, any reason that might push a man to the edge." He paused and turned towards us.

"It is clear that this man did not take his own life," he declared.

I looked at Inspector Lestrade standing beside me. Although attempting to conceal it, I detected a hint of frustration in the Scotland Yard detective's stiffening posture and the slight intake of breath. Holmes seemed to notice it too and a faint smile was visible across his face.

"How could a man suffering from Lymphedema in his left leg be able to stand on the desk, tie the noose from the ceiling and do this abhorrent deed?" Holmes added. I had read about the condition where damaged lymph nodes in the leg would cause it to swell and restrict a patient's movements. How my friend came to such a conclusion was beyond me. Seeing my perplexed expression, he indulged in his usual habit of explaining his methodical reasoning.

"Notice the tight fitting of the left trouser leg and the rather loose leg on the right. His condition is not so extreme, but the difference between the two is fairly noticeable. The worn sole of the left shoe, a substantial amount compared to the other, would indicate that he spent most of his time dragging his left foot wherever he walked."

Holmes had by now plunged into an unstoppable routine of presenting facts and, at each remark, indicating the details by pointing them out on the body.

"So he couldn't walk properly, but he could still have killed himself," insisted Lestrade.

"That may be Inspector, but how would you explain the brick dust?" my friend asked. I could see the bewilderment in the other's face: an expression that I had carried myself just moments earlier.

"There is a subtle but distinctive pattern formed on the desk by the fall of brick dust from the ceiling. The dust seems to have settled around an oval-shaped object and left an imprint on the surface of the desk. These same fragments can be found on the right side of the man's face." Holmes raised his left hand and pointed at a fine red hue on the neck of the victim just below the mask.

"Clearly the man was already dead before being hanged. He was laid on the desk by the culprits while they attached the rope to the ceiling and fixed the noose." He left the body and went to the desk. Bending down, he extracted his magnifying glass and took a closer look at the chipped edge.

"A foot has been pressed hard against the edge with considerable force. It is safe to conclude that one of the culprits assumed this position while hoisting the body up and slipping the noose over the victim's head."

I moved closer towards Holmes to look at the mark on the desk.

"Couldn't it still have been this same man who, unable to do so with his left leg, used his right to climb onto the desk and place the rope over his head?" I challenged. Sherlock Holmes smiled and stood up again.

"My dear Watson! Your stubbornness is just as remarkable as Scotland Yard's finest." He gave a sidelong look at Lestrade, who in turn made no attempt to conceal his annoyance.

"The chipped wood has two distinct edges which measure the width of the front curve of a man's heavy boot. Our poor man's shoe size fits within half of that mark, and is of a rectangular pattern rather than curved, which means that at least one of our culprits is someone of considerable size and stature with a large footprint."

"And the name A. V. Gordon?" I gestured at the wooden box.

"Inconsequential. At least, until we learn more about how the name of Horrigan Industries came to be in this room."

I was amazed at my friend's series of deductions and could not understand how, now that they were laid out so clearly, I had failed to come to the same conclusions. Yet, there was one point which I still did not entirely understand.

"Why do you think it was more than one murderer, Holmes?"

"Our victim is no more than five feet tall and yet, even someone of strength would find it almost impossible to hoist him up and attach the rope around his neck. Our culprit has had the assistance of a second individual." He approached the body and gently removed the mask that had been left on the face throughout our entire conversation.

"Now that we have laid out the facts, all that remains is to answer the Who and the Why," proclaimed Holmes, as he stepped backwards with the mask in his hand. The face behind the prop belonged to a middle-aged man with hard features and distinctively pale skin even allowing for the pallor of death. Assuming the crime had probably been committed during the night, there were distinctive characteristics that made no sense in my experience as a medical doctor. The purple hue round the wide eyes and the lopsided mouth were too pronounced, whilst the texture of the skin appeared too loose. Whatever distress caused this man to assume the face of death in such a short time, it seemed evident that he had been suffering from some prolonged illness.

As I looked away from that horrible image, I noticed Holmes bending over the desk and scrutinising the mask from every possible angle. His magnifying lens would enhance the hidden details he was surely hunting for.

"Pantaloon," Holmes mumbled, as he remained bent over the theatrical prop. I took a step forward, curious to have another look at the bizarre artefact.

"There is one final thing that you failed to notice Watson," he said suddenly, as if he had perceived I was observing his intense analysis of the mask. "The ability of sight may furnish you with many details, but there are other senses more powerful than what the eye beholds. When you came into this room you may have noticed the blazing fire and yet you failed to ask the most simple of questions." Sherlock Holmes stopped short and chuckled to himself. He turned away from the desk in an excitable manner and looked out through the window. It was at times like these that my companion demonstrated a lack of basic human interaction. While Lestrade and I, enraptured by his account, waited for an answer, Sherlock Holmes had walked from one window to the other, attempting to twist the handles up and down. The silence was accompanied by the occasional crackling of the logs in the fireplace.

"Well, Holmes? What question?" I finally broke out, unable to contain my anticipation. My companion halted his movement and slowly turned round.

"Why is the room so cold?" he asked.

I confess that his statement perplexed me. The room was warm but certainly not as hot as it should have been, given its small size and the relative intensity of the flames. Yet I suddenly recalled the chill I felt as I entered the room. It was not only the physical consequence of dread at the ghastly sight of death, but a frosty air had been lingering inside as if a gust of wind had blown in from the street outside. However, as Holmes had just proven, the windows were tightly shut.

"It is a basic scientific fact that the chemical combustion of fire in such a small space would generate a substantial amount of heat. Yet, upon our arrival, the room was as cold and damp as any London street at the moment." Inspector Lestrade and I both looked at the burning logs in the fire.

"There is of course the other matter," stated Holmes suddenly.

"What other matter?" I asked.

"Oranges." He sniffed deeply and exhaled. "There is an unmistakable aroma of citric acid commonly found in such fruits currently invading this room." He sniffed once more and paced round in a clockwise direction until he stopped beside us next to the door. I looked round and failed to spot the source of such a smell.

"And yet, no oranges in sight." smiled Holmes, reading my thoughts. "Frankly, had there been no body, I would have found this whole affair rather comical."

Yet his face soon turned serious as he gazed back at the mask on the desk. He walked slowly towards it and I noticed his deep penetrating eyes fixed upon the prop. I stood beside him, perceiving something more was amiss than the case of a dead man.

"What is it Holmes?" I asked.

"This room, Watson. This entire room is a lie."

With that, he buttoned his coat, walked out of the room and I followed him from the house onto the busy streets of London.

Sherlock Holmes walked in silence as we proceeded round the corner into the bustling life of Gilbert Street.

His pace was brisk and precise. I found myself struggling to catch up with my companion as he waded among the stream of pedestrians filling up the London walkways. Looking up at my side, I could see his eyes fixed straight ahead. His face was set with an expression that recalled a great mind at work, and instilled fear in anyone yet to come to light at the end of the case before him.

"The contents of that room were designed to test me. I need data," he proclaimed, as he rushed inside a telegraph office at the intersection between Orchard Street and Oxford Street. Having written down a few words on a piece of paper, Sherlock Holmes handed it over to the clerk and walked out again.

Calling for a cab, we headed back to our lodgings in Baker Street where my companion sat down in his favourite armchair next to the fireplace. Taking up his pipe from the mantelpiece and some tobacco from the inside of a slipper nearby, he proceeded to make a display of the finest smoke rings I had yet seen from him.

"Well Holmes, what's the next step?" I burst out, as we had remained silent for the best part of fifteen minutes. By then, the room was enveloped in a cloud of white smoke as my friend began puffing into his fifth serving.

"A criminal's art is his deception. Committing the crime is his mistake," he said, lowering his pipe and resting both hands on the arms of the chair.

"There are people who go to great lengths in order to impress and demonstrate their skill at what they do. Whoever designed the contents of that room in Weighhouse Street, has crafted a splendid piece of theatre designed to shock and throw anyone off the scent."

As often happened, Holmes seemed to have spoken his mind without attempting to simplify its contents so as to be comprehended by other human beings.

"You think someone staged the murder?" I inquired. Holmes rose sharply and reached for his great index book: that resource of data so essential to my companion's exploits. He flipped through the pages until he reached the *P* section.

"That mask, the one the victim wore," he said slowly as if to himself, whilst running his right forefinger down a long list on the page, "a curious object, wouldn't you say?"

"Bizarre and inappropriate. Only the most twisted of minds could have thought of such a heinous touch to an already horrible death," I replied, as the ghastly image of the grinning face came back to me. Holmes was still frowning over the page he had settled on. Suddenly, he walked across to me and handed over the bulky tome.

"I think the following text will be of utmost interest to you," he said, indicating the section with his finger, as I received the hefty book. Holmes had gone back to his armchair and closed his eyes, while I began reading aloud the short paragraph my friend had pointed at.

Pantaloon, or as it is more commonly known in its place of origin 'Pantalone', is a comedic figure in the theatrical scene born out of Italy during the 16th century. The Commedia Dell'Arte was characterised by improvised performances and masked characters. Pantaloon is most commonly associated with greed and the acquisition of money.

I re-read the passage in silence, feeling Holmes' uninterrupted gaze on me. "I still fail to see what the meaning of this theatre prop has in all of this," I finally declared with an exasperated sigh.

"The little details, Watson. The details on the canvas are what transform a painting into a masterpiece," my friend replied, "but even the most intricate works of art have flaws."

He leaped out of the chair and dashed across the room towards the front door.

A bell had rung and the unmistakable thud of footsteps rose from the staircase. As Holmes opened the door, in came a young boy of not more than twelve. His dishevelled and ragged appearance spoke of a homeless life among the rough streets of London.

"Your telegram, Mr Holmes," he said, as he handed over a piece of paper. The boy stood there looking expectantly at both of us, until my companion placed a coin in his hand and he sped off back out into Baker Street.

Sherlock Holmes opened the paper and chuckled. He handed it over and stood motionless on the spot. The following words were scribbled on the paper: 'Bielski. Beak Street'.

"What is the meaning of this, Holmes?" I asked, looking at the still composure of my companion.

"The noose tightens round our little case," he muttered. His eyes stared into the distance as if witnessing the coming of events not far off. I looked at him, wondering what clue or plan had formed in his head. He suddenly snapped out of his silent thoughts as if he felt my inquiring interest.

"Pardon my expression in such circumstances. I'll be back in a few hours." Seizing his hat and coat, he wound a scarf tightly round his neck. "Stay indoors Doctor and keep the fire roaring. It will be a bitter night."

It was just after noon and the sun shone joyfully over the city streets, lifting the fog and dispelling any shadows still concealed. Yet, even inside our cosy lodgings, the threat of a frosty afternoon persisted, so I took up my friend's advice and settled in the sitting-room next to the fire, reading a copy of Stevenson's *Strange Case of Dr Jekyll and Mr Hyde*. I was engrossed in the story but felt a sense of growing uneasiness as I was reminded of the brutal scene that had greeted me earlier that morning. Every now and then, my mind would dwell on the case at hand. No matter how hard I tried to find an explanation behind the gruesome crime, the missing elements and the hints from my friend's investigation, I ventured no further than what I had been witness to a few hours before: a terrible murder of an unknown man in an abandoned house. The monstrous elements of fiction I was reading felt only too real as I spent a good part of that day with the book in my hand, and by the time I had reached the final pages, it was already late in the afternoon.

Just before supper, Sherlock Holmes showed up. His spirited movements as he came up the steps indicated he had been successful in his endeavours. He took off his hat, coat and scarf, and sat down opposite me beside the fireplace. He was visibly excited and his eyes shifted constantly as if his mind was churning up complex analyses and inconceivable reasoning. Finally, my companion looked straight at me from across the room. The light outside had started to fade and the firelight reflected brightly in his keen dark hazel eyes.

"Watson, this evening I will be a murder victim."

I stood up, aghast and unable to comprehend the magnitude of what he had just said.

"What on earth are you saying Holmes?" I stammered.

"Pardon me Watson! It is a devious habit of mine to divulge fragments of information beyond the confines of my mind. I now realise that those at the receiving end are more at risk of drawing out the wrong conclusion from partial facts than the beauty of silence itself. Your concern for my well-being is admirable, but there is no cause for alarm. Threats to my safety are in the mind of many a criminal now finding themselves at the mercy of the justice system."

In all my adventures with Sherlock Holmes I had seen the veracity and the sophistication with which he had exposed murderers and thieves. A fury must have festered among the countless individuals now forced to live inside the suffocating walls of a prison cell. Revenge on the person who had brought their downfall would be a fitting consolation for them: the sense of satisfaction that punishment would be dealt out to Holmes as if to appease their own suffering. I now found these possibilities disconcerting, but my companion's light-hearted attitude gave me some comfort.

"I assure you Watson that my being another victim in this most fascinating case is but a little plan I have devised. I have had a productive day and, with the help of the good Inspector and yourself tonight, I shall expect the definite conclusion of this affair."

"Would you care to at least enlighten me on your progress? I have thought much, but cannot make ends meet with this case," I pressed him, knowing his usual way of retaining information till the very last minute. I wanted to know in some measure what he had gathered from the evidence he had found that morning.

Although Sherlock Holmes relished the opportunity to divulge all his thoughts once the case was complete, I could not help but notice a slight gleam in his eye that indicated he cherished my request for details on the investigation. He sat down in his armchair, took his briar pipe from the mantelpiece, struck a match and held it above the tobacco-filled bowl. As the scent of tobacco filled the air, he began his account. Meanwhile, I sat opposite him like an expectant child.

"Very well, Watson. Let us walk through some of the obvious facts in order. In an abandoned house, in a fairly quiet street, the body of a man is discovered, hanging from the ceiling of the study. A mask covers his face and the only clue as to an identity of sorts is a box with the name *A. V. Gordon* on it. We have already established that the man was already dead before he was hanged, as evidenced by the faint dust marks on the desk where his head had been resting. We further concluded that it had taken two men to hoist the body and hang it from the ceiling; an impossible task for one person, and any more than two would have been unnecessary. There was no visible evidence of any more footprints in the room other than those of the two culprits and ours. The damage to the desk was where one individual stepped in order to reach the ceiling and attach the rope, whilst the other hoisted the body into position."

I shifted in my armchair and leaned forward as Holmes began to venture into the mysteries of the murder that I had yet to discover.

"The body of the man, Watson," he continued, "you may have noticed the strange discolouration of the man's face."

"Yes," I replied, recalling the purple rings round the eyes, the skewed mouth, the elasticity of the skin, "as if an illness had plagued the man for many years. That would explain the odd occurrence of such extreme pallid features so short a time after death."

"Ah! But there may be another explanation for such an appearance. The mysterious scent of oranges, Watson!"

Again I recalled the strange presence of that smell in the room.

"What can we make of that?" my friend continued, "the eye is invaluable to the acquisition of details, but the mind has other tools equally critical in the successful endeavours of deduction. We, myself included, were all deceived by the citric scent invading the room, yet we could not find the source from which it emanated. That would lead us to conclude that the scent came with the body, rather than from any part of the house. However, there was a particular tinge to that smell, wholly alien to the savoury fruit. I read a monograph a few years ago about the variety of aromas produced by herbs." He paused for a moment and refilled his pipe, after which he continued his analysis.

"*Thymus citriodorus*, a citrus thyme with the distinct feature of smelling like lemons or oranges. This afternoon's investigation brought me to a little shop in Beak Street, just off Regent Street, specialising in the selling of this specific species of thyme; a family business owned by two Polish brothers by the name of Bielski. The herb itself is commonly used for disinfection, the lowering of blood pressure and other remedies from which the health of someone in need can benefit. Yet, given the state of the deceased, we can rule out any good intentions of preserving his health. Hence, we must conclude that the victim was previously inside the shop before he found himself in that house. Following this reasoning, it is simple enough to work out that the herb shop on Beak Street is being used for types of business transactions other than the mere selling and buying of thyme. I suspect that the two brothers have found it substantially more profitable too. They are men for hire, I would say. They receive information on potential victims to be properly disposed of. A most horrid affair of which we shall be exposing its every intricacy this evening."

I was astonished at the wealth of information he gleaned from the limited clues that seemed to haunt that house. Yet there were still many unanswered questions that I could think of.

"Holmes, why would they not attempt to conceal the body, rather than faking a suicide in plain sight. And what of the mask?" I felt my companion had all the answers at that point and I wanted to know more while his fit of giving them was on him.

"It is a custom among Polish gangs to place a mask on the body of a victim as a warning to any rival gangs attempting to outmanouver the dominant group. It would seem that we have a war between a number of criminal organisations in the midst of London, but that will have to wait for another time. Tonight, it is my intention to bring this trading business in Beak Street to an end and trap the culprits. Hence, I have sent news of my death via an acquaintance or two in the London criminal network to reach the ears of the Bielskis."

"So are we to seek out this shop and hope to apprehend the brothers there?" I inquired.

"Not at all! We are going back to the house in Weighhouse Street and lure the two men to the very same scene of the crime."

It was past seven o'clock when we left our lodgings and made our way back to Weighhouse Street. As we sat in the cab, shielding ourselves from the persistent cold that had returned at the setting of the sun, Holmes was in a most pleasant mood. His stern stares and quiet demeanour were replaced by a rare smile and a talkative disposition.

"The lie of the room has been exposed, Watson. The truth is confirmed and the evidence needed will be given depending on my skills as an actor," he began, as we rattled our way past the shops and offices in Oxford Street.

"What lie, Holmes? Have you discovered the reason for that poor man's death?" I leaned forward towards my companion, intrigued at the unfolding explanations of the case.

"The victim's death is irrelevant, for as far as I am able to discern, no murder has been committed."

I confess that amid the noises of the busy street and the constant rhythm of the horse's hooves, I was adamant I had misheard my friend's remark.

Sherlock Holmes smiled as he perceived the confusèd look on my face. "The poor man had been dead for days before we ever entered that house. There was even that gash on the wall where the body was dragged from outside," he confirmed.

"How is that possible?" I exclaimed, "the discovery was made only this morning and before that the house seems to have been empty for years."

"The death of a person can occur elsewhere from where their body is laid to rest. It is our task to fashion the chain, link by link, and discover the How and the Why of the matter."

"So he did not die in the house?"

"Certainly not! That was mere theatrical dressing. Ah! but here we are at our destination."

Before I had time to press my inquiries further at this remarkable turn of events, we alighted from the cab and walked a short distance towards the abandoned house. There was no remarkable difference in appearance at that time of day. The street itself seemed to have been left almost uninhabited since the morning. Very few people moved along it and with the deepening dark, it felt all the more cut off from the rest of the city, giving a sense of threat and foreboding.

I followed Holmes as he stepped onto the pavement and approached the half-open door. My initial enthusiasm to follow in his pursuit of resolving the case began to wane as a sense of discomfort grew in me. That morning, under the newly-risen sun, that decrepit house had left a mark on me. Now, in the fading light, the peeling paint on the surface of the door reminded me of the dark corridor with the worn carpet and the room in which the grisly discovery was made.

As my friend pushed the door open, a faint light became visible and dispelled the many shadows invading the entrance.

"Right on time Mr Holmes!" spoke a voice from inside. It sounded familiar, but the sudden greeting had startled me. My friend was in front as we entered, and his broad shoulders concealed the source of the voice. As we proceeded further, the small shape of Inspector Lestrade came into view. Behind him, each one carrying a lit candle, were two police constables.

"Inspector, good of you to join us." Sherlock Holmes walked past Lestrade and into the room, taking off his hat and coat. I followed him and looked once more into that place of nightmares. The body had obviously been removed by the police and the room looked as ordinary as any other, except for its shabby state. With the dark outside now complete, it looked even more sinister. Although no man was strung up from the ceiling, the memory of that image could not fade away and the dancing shadows produced by the candles made me feel uneasy. There were no burning logs in the fireplace and the room felt humid and cold. That strange smell of oranges, now faint, was still detectable.

"Have you brought the prop?" asked Holmes.

"As instructed," replied the inspector, producing a familiar Pantaloon mask and handing it over to him.

"And the whistle?" he added, as one of the police constables gave my companion a small cylindrical piece of metal.

"Excellent! Now, if you wouldn't mind concealing yourselves in the shadows further down the corridor, the play is about to begin." Unaware of my companion's next stage of the plan, I was escorted out by the Scotland Yard inspector. Taking one last look back into the room, I glimpsed Holmes putting on the mask and sitting on the chair at the desk, whilst laying the top half of his body on its surface. He was evidently assuming a similar position to that of the dead man before he had been hanged from the ceiling.

Together with Inspector Lestrade and the two police constables, I hid at the opposite end of the corridor. Having left the two burning candles in the room with Holmes, we found ourselves in total darkness just within sight of the front door. We were crouching next to each other, surrounded by musty and mouldy smells.

During that long vigil, where I could discern a gentle light streaming out of the room, I kept wondering what Holmes had in mind and why he had assumed the role of a dead man. I was completely oblivious towards a conclusive resolution to this most bizarre case. Over an hour passed since we had settled in the shadows and during that time I could hear Inspector Lestrade's deep breathing next to me.

It must have been past eight o'clock when suddenly I thought I heard a scraping noise coming from outside the front door. I felt, rather than saw, the others beside me stiffen, indicating that it was not my imagination. The door was pushed open and two men walked in. They appeared to be wearing dark clothing, which made it difficult to discern them clearly. They both wore caps and, as they walked in, made a dragging noise as their heavy boots scraped along the carpet. One appeared to be burly and of considerable strength, whilst the other was smaller in stature but still fairly well-built. The two men headed into the room and began making much clamour. It felt like we had been there for hours, hearing but being unable to comprehend what was going on, and where, in all that hustle and bustle, my friend was to be found. Finally, the sounds seemed to die down and more light appeared to emanate from inside. The distinctive sound of a rope being uncoiled could be heard, along with grunts from one of the intruders: deep intakes of breath as he seemed to be shifting a large object across the room. The two men spoke briefly to each other. From where we hid, I could faintly hear their conversation, but it was evident that they were talking in a foreign language. Suddenly, there was a stir in the room and the brief interlude came to an end.

The large object was being shifted into position again and the presumed rope being used for some purpose. I was just about to stand up and run to the aid of my friend when a sharp whistle call came down the corridor. Lestrade and the two constables were up in no time and leaped forward towards the room. I followed instantly, with the light growing stronger as I came to the door. Fearing the worst as I plunged into the room, I saw the police officers catching hold of two men in dark clothing. Lestrade was assisting in holding down the stronger of the two. One had been tying a noose from the ceiling and the other had just let go of Holmes. My friend looked up at me and smiled. The mask had fallen off during the scuffle and in his mouth he still held the whistle with which he had called for aid. There was also a noticeable difference in the room lighting. Whilst the candles had been extinguished, the fireplace was roaring once again with that green tinge to the flames.

"Well, let's hope that's the closest I'll ever get to the gallows," remarked my companion, in his usual way. He walked forward, putting on his coat again and pointed at the two men still struggling and cursing in their own language. As they were being held by the officers from Scotland Yard, I perceived that each of the two bore a small tattoo on their necks with the image of a stick inside a circle.

"Watson, may I present to you the Bielski brothers. Herb traders by day and body snatchers by night. Caught in the act of trying to dispose of my body in a rather fanciful way."

"We'll be off then, Mr Holmes," Lestrade grunted. The man he was holding gave a sudden jolt to free himself, but the inspector gripped him firmly.

"These two have plenty to answer for at Scotland Yard."

"Good night Inspector," replied Holmes, as the two men were escorted away.

Having exposed the culprits, Holmes and I made our way back to Baker Street, seeking the warm comfort of our lodgings. The fire was still burning brightly, and it struck me how different our study looked in its light compared to the room in Weighhouse Street. It made the whole case feel unearthly and, although we had apprehended the men responsible, I still had many unresolved questions to ask. Holmes seemed aware of this as he instantly settled in his armchair and lit up his pipe. I sat down opposite him and huddled close to the fireplace. He looked at me deeply, as if recalling the events that had brought him to this moment.

"This case, Watson, has been of utmost interest. It played on the mind and the senses and almost threw me off scent." He re-positioned himself in the armchair as if to dispel such an outrageous thought before continuing.

"It was evident that, although the Bielski brothers were behind the whole affair, they are certainly not murderers. The man, who is indeed the A. V. Gordon from Horrigan Industries, was dead before he found himself posed so fancifully in that room. You noticed the pale skin and the bizarre characteristics that riddled his face. Those were not the marks of a recent illness that plagued the man but rather the effects of oncoming decomposition following death by natural causes." Holmes accelerated his puffs as he delved further into the case. I sat silent, struck by the sudden twist of facts which at first seemed to be so obviously pointing in a different direction.

"Mr Albert Victor Gordon was the general secretary at Horrigan Industries until a year ago, before he found himself at the centre of a financial scandal. The newspapers were riddled with stories of his fraudulent actions and the high profits he had gained. Fortunately for him, with the help of a skillful lawyer he managed to elude prison. This success naturally attracted the attention of the criminal underworld and Mr Gordon became involved with some very dangerous people. His most recent endeavour, however, had brought him into close contact with the Zawisza gang: a modest organisation made up of Polish immigrants, whose specialty is in the art of large scale robberies.

"Undoubtedly, Mr Gordon's alliance with them was to his benefit at first, but ultimately he realised that he had found himself out of his depth.

"From the signs on his right leg, his Lymphedema condition had only emerged a few months ago but was quickly debilitating him, and he knew that death would soon be knocking at his door. So he devised a plan to ward off any of the Zawiszas from claiming his fraudulent wealth. During the scandal, the newspapers had reported that Gordon had a wife and daughter. The only way to safeguard his money for the well-being of his family would be to seek help from the Zawisza's fiercest enemies. Yes, in desperation, our protagonist sought to deflect attention by attracting it. A commendable attempt, if dangerously foolish.

"He therefore found the services of the Bielski brothers, both of whom had been members of the Kijek gang and bitter rivals of the Zawiszas. The inked symbol of a small walking stick on the side of their necks removed any doubt as to their former allegiance."

"Why former?" I abruptly put in. I was so enraptured by Holmes' account that my mind had audibly proclaimed that sudden pressing query like an instinctive reflex.

"The edges of the images were well refined, eliminating any doubt that the ink was expertly applied to the skin. Yet, the ink itself was much faded and, although the brothers had had it for quite some time, there were clear signs of abrasion all round the area, as if rigorous scrubbing had recently taken place."

Sherlock Holmes paused for a moment until he refilled his pipe and lit the contents. "The Kijek gang leaves its mark by placing a mask on all its victims, as a warning to any other rival groups not to meddle in their affairs. The Bielski brothers obviously knew this and agreed with Albert Gordon to use this same technique upon his death by staging his suicide, thereby warning any Zawiszas against interfering with Gordon's wealth and throwing the police off the scent. The abandoned house to be used for this illusion was an old meeting place of the Kijek gang. The body of Albert Gordon in that decrepit place would further reinforce the false story of financial trouble. It was only a matter of time before Gordon's eventual death led to the brothers setting up the room in that house. I am certain that their original pact consisted of the immediate display of the body, but the risky business of drawing attention to themselves forced them to postpone their initial plan. They had to find a place to store the corpse and only their shop allowed for the best concealment until the time was right. This resulted in the accumulation of the citric scent on the body and the first clue that brought us to the unravelling of this exquisite little case. Inadvertently, the scent helped to cover up any smell of the decomposition process."

"You have my utmost praise, Holmes. That was simply extraordinary, but one thing escapes me. What was the reason for the room being so cold with that roaring fire in the fireplace?"

"Ah! A delightful combination of methyl alcohol and boric acid, the effects of which produce what is known as cool flame," declared my friend. "The chemical reaction creates a fire that burns less keenly and at significantly lower temperatures than a normal blaze, and produces a distinctive green hue. This was carried out by the Bielski brothers in line with their old gang's custom: signalling from the inside of a house that their intended victim had been successfully dealt with."

"Well, that seems to be the end of the affair," I added, leaning back in my chair with a sense of satisfaction at the conclusion of the case.

"Quite right, Watson. Now draw closer to this real fire and keep the cold at bay," said my friend.

The Wooden Diamond

"I am in need Watson," proclaimed Sherlock Holmes.

"Absolutely not," I replied coldly, eyeing him from behind the newspaper I had been reading.

"A mere seven-per-cent solution, as discussed." He leaned forward in his armchair and reached out towards his syringe case on the mantelpiece.

"Holmes!"

"I need sustenance!" he whined.

"What you need is rest," I retorted. It could often be exasperating talk trying to convince the brilliant mind of Sherlock Holmes to do ordinary tasks. It had been several months since the events of *The Hanging Man*, and the number of clients making their way into our Baker Street lodgings had dwindled over the past few weeks. This, however, did not stop Sherlock Holmes from staying up for endless nights, carrying out experiments or spending hours in the dark London streets looking for means to keep his mind active. His need for work was like an engine in need of fuel.

"Stagnation Watson! The worst of enemies," he cried. Leaping out of his chair he headed towards the kitchen. On one of the tables was a curious display of laboratory equipment: test tubes, a Bunsen burner, pipettes and a colourful combination of glass bottles containing Sherlock Holmes' fermenting chemical experiments.

The burner was lit and a crystal-like substance had been left boiling in a flask for the best part of the morning. Holmes approached it with caution and bent down to examine the bubbling fluid at eye level. I observed his movements from behind my newspaper, intrigued by what he was working on. My medical background piqued my interest into the many experiments carried out by my friend. A sigh of frustration soon flowed back into the sitting-room.

"What is it you are doing with that?" I nodded towards the boiling liquid. Holmes had now come back and sat dejectedly in his armchair, the formidable persona of the consulting detective reduced to a child fuming over spoilt play.

"Testing the endurance of phosphorus pentoxide. I'm writing a monograph on the preservation of nutritive particles in humid regions." He gave a sidelong look at the equipment. "But it'll be a few more hours. In the meantime, I'm bound to this chair with a brain screaming for action." He sighed once more and turned towards the syringe he had been eyeing earlier. He sat there, motionless, as if some restraint was yet battling within him to control the need for consumption.

Just at that moment, we heard the distinctive ring of the front door bell followed by the footsteps of a visitor climbing up the stairs; the melodious sound of a potential client. I could see the subtlest hint of exaltation in my friend's face as he straightened himself up and gazed at the entrance. In walked a man whose appearance gave me the impression of a young gentleman not more than thirty years of age. His attire was neat but not too sophisticated. He appeared just over five feet in height, with a clean-shaven face and bright green eyes. Upon his chubby frame, he wore a pair of dark brown trousers which bore several stains of different hues and sizes, not least two dark blue blotches round his right knee. Over his shoulders was a long, dark overcoat, slightly weather-stained and worn at the cuffs. His face also bore the marks of an exhausted individual.

The staircase leading up to our lodgings only consisted of a single flight of stairs, yet the man standing in the doorway was visibly flushed: breathing heavily with his mouth open, looking at both of us in turn. The cause of his predicament might have been the rather large box he was carrying in his arms. Whatever contents lay inside, it generated a substantial amount of weight, so much so that the man suddenly raised the box to re-position his hands and get a better grip.

"Mr Holmes?" he inquired, amid his heavy breathing.

"My good sir. Pray, sit down." Sherlock Holmes leaped from his chair, walked towards our visitor and gestured towards the sofa. The change in my friend's behaviour was impressive. Sensing the potential arrival of a client, he burst forth with an energy and a vitality that belied his state of misery a few moments before. As it turned out, the case put forward by our guest would be of particular interest and concern to the mind of London's finest consulting detective.

"Might we know the reason as to why you sought us on such a wonderful day, and have been dragged away from your pregnant wife and young child?" proclaimed my friend.

Our visitor sat silent with his eyes and mouth wide open. Even I, accustomed to my friend's exceptional deductive skills, could not comprehend how he could have possibly guessed the man's personal affairs down to the pregnancy of his wife. Holmes perceived the incredulity on both our faces and pressed on.

"A girl perhaps?" he added, with a subtle smile across his face.

"Holmes! How on earth can you possibly tell?" I objected, feeling as baffled as the stranger himself. My friend chuckled.

"It is simplicity itself, Watson. My good sir, the ring on your left finger is sufficient to denote your marriage, whilst your attire bears concerns for pleasing the public eye. No disrespect, but behind your combination of clothing there is clearly a woman's touch. Yet, no caring wife would allow her husband to leave the house with stained and worn trousers. So it is obvious to the simplest of minds that whilst you have been duly guided on your attire, there has been a lack of attention to detail caused by some predicament or other. Illness is excluded as you would not have left your house to come to me on some other matter as evidenced by the box you are now holding. Something much more exciting, but nonetheless taxing, is currently occupying you and your wife. The dark rings round your eyes are enough to indicate a considerable lack of sleep brought about by anxiety and the earnest safety for your family. Additionally, you display a distinctive smudge of red powdered graphite on your right knee, the result of a crayon as commonly used by a child. To further substantiate this, there's a piece of paper protruding from your front coat pocket. The wording is much faded, but the printed monochrome insignia is quite distinctive:

Fairyland Toy Shop

You fear for the safety of your family, which is why you have done the correct thing and come to seek my advice."

"And the fact that he has a daughter?" I inquired, still trying to comprehend the wealth of information we had been inundated with.

"A devious diversion from my usual methodical process, but it was a mere educated guess."

Holmes had concluded his deductions. From the bewildered expression on our client's face, it was evident that my friend had correctly identified all parameters with typical exactness.

"Right on all accounts," said the man, reeling in disbelief. "Pardon me sir, I came to you on my way to work. My name is Eldridge. Thomas Eldridge, sir. Mr Newell from Goodge Street said your expertise would be able to assist me in my plight." Our client's rapid breathing was slowing down, but during his introduction, his constant intake of breath was accompanied by a wheezing sound. He also clutched at the box lying on his knees. Holmes had sat back down in his armchair, with his elbows resting on its arms and his fingers touching together.

"Roger Newell," proclaimed Holmes. He opened his eyes and gazed deeply at Mr Eldridge. "Ah, yes. A trifling crisis I helped avert for him some months ago." He maintained his posture with his hands together.

"Now pray, begin your account so that we may alleviate you of your predicament. My phosphorus pentoxide experiment is far from completion." Holmes glanced once more at the kitchen. The contents of the flask on the burner were still bubbling viciously.

"It's this thing," began Thomas Eldridge, slightly raising the closed box as evidence. He paused and took another deep breath, "this object I keep finding." He stopped again and then, with some difficulty, continued.

"I've had a quiet life Mr Holmes. I have the privilege of taking care of my wife and child as you quite rightly pointed out. My business as a tradesman has seen better days, but I cannot complain. We manage a living somehow and I have never had any serious trouble from customers or debtors. If there's one thing I learnt from my father, it's that of being as honest a man as anyone else. I've crafted ornaments out of wood since I was a lad. People used to marvel at my skill and that's what got me into setting up my own shop and selling these trinkets and sculptures for people to fill their shelves and decorate their homes with. Ten years I have been in Streatham Street, attending to my shop. Since then, I've met my wife and started a family. We made the most of what life gave us and were content with what we had. Yet my business has started to decline. Fewer customers walk through the door every day. Still, I work hard to sustain my family during these difficult times.

"Everything seemed to take a turn for the worse ever since we had that visitor to my shop. He showed up one morning, gaunt and with a wide-brimmed hat over his head, so it was difficult for me to say how old he really was. He wore a soiled leather coat with mud-stained boots. On his bent back he carried a small bag that dangled from side to side as he limped his way into the shop. His unsavoury appearance made me feel uneasy so I met him on the doorstep.

" 'Be off! We don't want any beggars round here.' I was rather aggressive in tone. Perhaps it was the recent thefts that had taken place a few streets away. I was on guard for any troublemakers, and this new visitor struck me as suspicious. I waved my hand in front of his face and stood where I was, blocking the way.

" 'Begging your pardon, my good sir.' I confess I was quite surprised by his reply. His voice belied his appearance. It was soft and clear, with a distinctive note to it. 'I am here on an honest request with money for your time,' he continued. He produced a handful of coins from his bag and displayed them as evidence of his goodwill. I relented from my hostile attack, but kept my guard, allowing the man to walk inside and make his request at the counter, as is usual practice with all my customers. What he required was simple enough. He asked for a decorative frame in the shape of a diamond."

"A moment Mr Eldridge," intervened my friend. "Did he say what he intended to use it for?"

"I don't usually ask my clients about their intention for the objects I make, and this particular one seemed as normal a request as any other," replied our guest.

"Thank you Mr Eldridge, please continue." My friend resumed his original position by leaning back in the armchair with his eyes closed and his fingertips touching once again. Meanwhile, our client proceeded with his account.

"Having been given the necessary details and dimensions of the piece – which, I must say, were rather precise

– I instructed him to pick up the finished work on the following Thursday. Being a Monday and with clients not a common occurrence at that time, it was only a few days' work of woodcarving before I would have completed the frame. He thanked me and paid me in advance, before he limped back towards the front door, leaving me quite perplexed as to his odd behaviour.

"Odd or not, I was nonetheless glad of the income – little though it was – and soon started labouring on the desired piece. I enjoy my work Mr Holmes, and some days more than others. It depends on the intricacy of the piece and the mood I am in. Suffice to say, this proved quite a challenge and kept me engaged for the best part of two days. On Wednesday, I placed the finished piece in a box on a nearby shelf next to the counter, to be picked up the following morning.

"Oddly enough, Thursday was rather an unexpectedly busy day with two or three clients asking for services which would keep me busy for the whole of the following week. One thing drove out another and I completely forgot about the strange man and the wooden frame lying on the shelf, gathering dust. It was a good month later that I happened to notice the box and remember its contents.

"I recalled the strange encounter with the limping man in my shop. Why would someone request my work, pay for it in advance and then fail to pick it up? These were the questions that haunted me. I had no means to get in touch with the man as he had left no particulars. I began to wonder whether some ill had befallen him, which prevented him from claiming the frame. Yet, as I said, I could do nothing at that point so I decided I would leave it there until the man had a mind to come for it. There it has lain on the dusty shelf ever since."

"And am I correct in thinking you have brought this object for us to see?" stated Holmes, as if finishing Mr Eldridge's sentence. He gestured at the box still within the tight grip of our client.

"That's correct, Mr Holmes. This is what I've been talking about." He loosened his hold and pushed the box forward. Cautiously, he raised the lid and lifted the contents within. In his hands our client held a most remarkable object: an intricately carved frame in the shape of a diamond with four angular points. It measured no more than a foot from point to point, top to bottom and side to side. It was of a light brown colour, highly-polished and emitting a musty smell.

My friend took the object in his hands and placed it on the surface of the table. He slid off his armchair and fell down on his knees, bending down in close proximity to the intricate design.

It was certainly a most unique piece and not a typical wall mirror, as there was no glass attached to the frame, for in the centre of the wooden diamond was an exquisite carving of two little angels facing each other: one pointing, the other kneeling in submission. A floral pattern like an interlaced ivy went round the entire length of the frame.

"A most singular piece, wouldn't you say, Watson?" remarked my friend, as he placed the object inside the box and laid it on the table before sitting back in his armchair.

"It certainly makes for an odd request. I have never seen such an item decorating the walls of even the most eccentric households. What could it all mean?" I asked.

"That will soon be aided by Mr Eldridge's continuation of his fascinating account." He turned to our client, who was left somewhat bewildered by our brief conversation.

"Something has happened to force you to seek my services, has it not?" he added.

Our client remained silent, gazing at the box in front of him. A subtle change had come over his face. He winced and swallowed, shifting uncomfortably on the sofa. He was fiddling with his fingers, with his mind clearly far away from that room. I glanced at Holmes sitting opposite me. For a moment, my friend raised his eyebrows and then settled into a stern expression.

"Well?" asked my companion, "is that not why you are here?"

Mr Eldridge looked up at both of us, as if snapping out of a deep thought.

"What? Oh yes, my apologies gentlemen. It's been a rather rough few days," he replied. He gave a slight nervous laugh as he said so and, with much hesitation, continued his account.

"It was last Saturday, after yet another uneventful day, when I closed the shop in the evening and made my way home. I prefer walking to taking a cab, Mr Holmes. A good walk is always better than a shilling or two less. Besides, it takes me only fifteen minutes from my shop in Streatham Street to my humble dwelling in Woburn Place, just past Russell Square. The walk back was a quiet one, with as fine an evening as you could wish for."

Sherlock Holmes' stern expression remained unchanged and whilst he nodded throughout our client's account, I could see that he perceived more than was being said. Our client proceeded in laying out the details of his story.

"You should know, Mr Holmes, that as soon as you turn round the corner from Russell Square, my house comes into view, but is partly hidden by the tall shrubs and overgrown hedges along the façade. A single light in that dark street is visible, emerging from behind the glass panes of my front door. On any other night, I would see the shadow of my lovely wife moving about inside the house, but on this particular evening, even as I crossed the street, I could see an odd shape covering much of the emerging light. As I approached the door, a chill ran down my spine and I stopped dead in my tracks. The unmistakable features of the wooden diamond I had laboured on were faintly visible. I could not comprehend how the object found itself at my house when I could clearly recall seeing the box in my shop. My first thought was that this was not the same object but one which bore some strikingly similar features. However, as I approached my front door, I could not help but realise that the frame hanging there was the same one I had produced: the carving technique, the smooth design, the intricate details, all were clearly indicative of my own work. Images of the old man with his bent back rushed through my head.

"Although I was certain that this was the same object I had been tasked with, I could not help rushing back through the dark London streets to my shop. Seized by an incomprehensible state of fear, I took the box down from the shelf and opened it. I was greeted by nothing more than the bottom of the box itself. The object hanging on my front door had, without a doubt, come from this box. That night I lay in bed unable to find rest. The old man haunted my thoughts and the riddle of how the object had seemingly travelled on its own drove me mad. I spent all of Sunday in an anxious state. On Monday, I went back to the shop and opened the box once more. The wooden diamond was still there where I had placed it back on Saturday evening. That day passed slowly, but finally I found myself walking back home in the evening. As I hurried through the streets, recalling the mysterious circumstances under which the old man had made such an odd request, and his failure to show up, I discerned once again the unmistakable diamond shape on my front door. I recoiled in horror as I felt the world spinning round me at the sinister impossibility of this occurrence. I ran up to my door and sure enough the same wooden frame I had left inside the box in my shop was there in front of me. Two days later and I haven't slept a wink, Mr Holmes. After Monday evening, there were no more appearances and the object was secure in its box on the top shelf in my shop in Streatham Street."

"How high is the shelf?" asked Holmes bluntly. Both Eldridge and I looked at my friend with intriguing looks, wondering at the oddness of the question after hearing such a singular account.

"I fail to see how ..." began our client.

"The height of the shelf on which you keep the box with the wooden diamond," interjected Holmes.

"I should say just over six feet," replied Thomas Eldridge after some deliberation.

"Excellent! And therefore you have obviously come to seek my help in clearing up this most mysterious affair," added Sherlock Holmes.

"That's right sir. For the safety of my family, I would have you look into this matter to see whether this strange occurrence presents any immediate threat. As I said Mr Holmes, I'm a simple man who has never made any enemies. I lead a fair life and whoever wishes any ill upon myself or those I love must surely be of an unstable mind. I beg you Mr Holmes, help me in this plight!"

I sorely pitied the poor soul who sat there in our study, begging my friend for help. I looked over at my companion who sat still in his armchair, looking across at our client with those steadfast eyes and contemplating matters beyond our imagination.

"I'm afraid there's very little to go on Mr Eldridge," proclaimed Holmes, after a moment of silence. "It would seem that this incident is nothing more than a sophisticated joke."

Holmes' discouraging words had forced our client to look helplessly at us in turn.

"But this thing, Mr Holmes! This impossible thing!" he gestured at the open box on the table. "I came to you as soon as I found this note."

My friend was on the point of standing up when he was forced back down. Our client had hastily pulled out a crumpled piece of paper from his trouser pocket and presented it to us.

Holmes and I leaned forward, as my companion extended his arm and took the note in his hand.

As he opened it, the wrinkled paper displayed a short handwritten message in smudged ink:

The Time has come.

"What could that possibly mean?" I asked.

Holmes sniffed, and after having examined the paper with his usual intricate manner, folded it again.

"May I keep this?" he asked, and following the approval of our client, he placed it inside his waistcoat pocket.

"Mr Eldridge, this new development has certainly enhanced a fascinating account. I shall endeavour to help you in your matters and provide a satisfactory resolve to your worries. Might I suggest we meet at your shop this afternoon at 3 o'clock to begin our investigation?"

"Most certainly Mr Holmes." Our client stood up with a beaming smile and extended his hand to my friend, shaking it vigorously with excitement.

"Now pray," said Holmes, as he stood up in turn, "you can't possibly leave us without taking a look at the experiment I'm conducting. Watson, will you do the honours and escort Mr Eldridge to the kitchen and explain the nature of my scientific analysis?" he said, as he looked at me with a strange smile.

I confess that the request was an odd one and took me by surprise. I had hardly grasped the process of the bubbling liquid myself, so Holmes' desire for me to show our client the experiment in progress was rather out of character. Our client was equally flummoxed by the suggestion as he stood there with half a smile on his face. Yet, I duly obliged and rose to conduct Eldridge into the kitchen, leaving Holmes in the study as he proceeded to light up his pipe.

After a few minutes trying to recall our conversation in the morning, and guiding our client through the maze of laboratory equipment that filled the kitchen table, I escorted him back to the study, to find Holmes closing the lid on the wooden box and bringing it over to its owner.

"I trust to your welcome this afternoon Mr Eldridge," said he with a smile.

"Most certainly Mr Holmes," replied our client, as he made his way out and down the stairs.

We heard the footsteps fade away as we sat back down in the study.

"A rather puzzling affair, wouldn't you say Holmes?" I inquired after a few moments of silence. My companion had resumed his position on the armchair whilst puffing away at his pipe. He said nothing but raised his eyebrows as if dismissing the whole thing.

"Surely you must consider the extraordinary circumstances of this object's appearances," I insisted.

Sherlock Holmes sighed and amid a billow of smoke, removed the pipe from his mouth and opened his eyes.

"There is nothing more tedious, Watson, than an account that barely makes sense and lacks detail," he replied, with his usual sharpness. He stood up and placed the pipe back on the mantlepiece. "Whatever this case has in store for us, we'll soon see it through in a few hours."

He walked out of the study and returned presently with a long and rather large coat over his shoulders. His hands, pushed deep in its pockets, were wrapped close round his waist. His posture was bent and with a hat over his head, he was unrecognisable to anyone except those who knew him very well. Though spring in London could be unpredictable, the weather had been fair for the last couple of days. My friend's behaviour, first at the sudden interest in showing our client his ongoing experiment and now with his attire, struck me as highly unsuitable to the great persona of the consulting detective.

"Is something the matter Holmes? You seem rather peculiar today," I asked as he made his way to the door.

"Nonsense Watson! I'll be back in a few hours," he uttered, and dashed out into the teeming life of Baker Street.

It had only been two hours since his unexpected exit, when Sherlock Holmes returned in a most pleasant mood. The large coat was gone and his behaviour quite the opposite to the gloomy and oppressive manner of that morning.

"It would seem you have been successful in your endeavours." I lowered the book which I had been reading as I saw Holmes make his way into the study.

"Hush, Watson. None of that now," he replied. Picking up his violin, he proceeded to play the most exquisite rendition of Bach's Adagio, and no further words were uttered until it was time for us to make our way to Thomas Eldridge's shop in Streatham Street.

"Welcome gentlemen! Please come in." We had been greeted by Mr Eldridge just outside his workplace. The shop itself showed clear signs of old age, with its battered façade and faded wood. The window panes were dusty and much stained, whilst the sign over the door bore faint lettering that spelled out the name of the shop.

Eldridge's Wood Carving
Est. 1877

As we walked inside, I was instantly aware of the stuffiness of the place. The tang of humid sawdust permeated the air upon our arrival, which further increased the state of gloom the shop already bore. Two small lanterns glowed at the far end of the workspace, but the weak flames were a poor beacon amid the labyrinth of wooden creations scattered around the shop. Half-finished statues and highly intricate ornaments filled every corner. Our client may not have had much success in his line of work, but his talent was undisputed. Here lay many works of art which had remained hidden from the public eye, and were bound to lie hidden in the dark, collecting dust.

I remarked my fascination to our host, who was delighted with the compliment and instantly took the initiative to take me round to observe some of his current projects. Holmes, meanwhile, plunged into a series of critical analyses of the counter and the shelves behind, which were situated between the two burning lanterns.

At one point, looking away from a fine example of a wooden bust of Queen Victoria, I happened to notice my friend's close inspection of the top shelf where lay the box containing the wooden diamond. With the help of his convex lens, he scrutinised every angle of the space before completely satisfying himself, then proceeded to walk behind the counter to where the writing area had been established, and bent down to its surface with his lens. He analysed everything in minute detail, from the stained and dusty pile of blank papers, to the dip pen which had rolled to rest against the ink bottle. Nothing could escape the eagle-eyed detective.

"Now Mr Eldridge, I believe that you have placed the box with the wooden diamond back on that shelf." Holmes pointed to the spot behind him that he had just examined.

"Yes Mr Holmes, it's been there since I came back from our meeting this morning," replied our client.

"Good. Let us leave it where it is and perhaps we can make our way to your house."

Thomas Eldridge's face turned into a state of confusion in response to my companion's request, "My house, sir?"

"Indeed. Whilst leaving the object here, we will take the same route on foot as you have done, and see what we shall see," remarked Holmes with a distinctive smirk on his face.

"Yes, yes of course. That's quite sensible," mumbled Eldridge.

Having turned off the lanterns and secured the lock on the shop's front door, we proceeded to head towards 31, Woburn Place.

The sun was still high up above the roofs around Russell Square Gardens, when we arrived in front of our client's house. The road itself was lined by two rows of battered houses facing each other. Thomas Eldridge's abode was equally shabby, which further highlighted the poor state of his business.

"But that's not possible!" Our client had rushed across the street towards his house standing behind a dishevelled hedge with overgrown shrubs. We followed after him and soon realised the reason for his predicament. Upon the upper part of the main door, where the dirty paned glass was affixed, there hung that same wooden diamond which had so perplexed our visitor that morning. He stood in the path just in front of the door. His figure, bent with anxiety, turned round to face us, wild terror in his eyes. "The diamond was in the box! I didn't …" Thomas Eldridge stopped short in his exclamation.

"It would seem that my trap has caught the prey at last," remarked Sherlock Holmes with his usual calm demeanour, as we walked up to the stricken man. He put one hand on the other's shoulder.

"I think it's time you give up your little ruse Mr Eldridge," he said quietly.

I confess that I could not fathom the circumstances which led to the resolution of this bizarre case, but I was soon to find out. Upon Holmes' suggestion, we all went inside the house and having sat down in his hospitable – yet far from dainty – living room, our client gave his confession.

"It was the money that did it. That was what pushed me to do all this." He looked longingly at his pregnant wife, who had sat down beside him. She knew less than Holmes and I did of this whole affair, and much of what her husband confessed she discovered there for the first time. Her face was that of a confused and betrayed woman, yet she clutched his hand with a firmness which demonstrated a sense of pity and understanding within her.

"I've already made reference to my financial situation, Mr Holmes. No doubt you saw for yourself from the state of my shop which, although filled with all my work, was devoid of any customers. It was therefore a blessing when one day I found this old man coming into my shop and commissioning that object which has given me so much moral anguish. Mr Holmes, I must confess that I was not completely honest with my account to you this morning."

I looked over at my friend who nodded gently, as if he had long perceived the deception.

"A few weeks after the object was due to be picked up, the old man returned. He looked exactly as he had done before, with his soft voice and the bag over his back. He asked for the wooden diamond and after having praised my talent, he handed it back to me and made another request."

Our client shifted in his chair and proceeded with his strange tale.

" 'A simple fabrication and altering of fact is all I ask.' He said this as he placed an open envelope on the counter. It contained several banknotes, such an amount which I had never seen before me. I looked at him uneasily. His rough and sinister appearance was already unnerving, but this new development had completely upset me. I wanted him out of the shop and gave him back the envelope with the money. I was a respectable man and one of honour. I was certainly not going to be part of any strange game he was playing.

" 'It's a pity,' he said as he walked towards the front door. 'Such a sum is hard to come by these days, especially in these circumstances.' He looked round the shop with sarcastic pity on his face, as if he could perceive the lack of business which plagued me. He waved at me with the envelope in his hand and opened the door to leave. It was at that moment that a rush of anxiety swelled in me. I thought of my wife, my daughter and my unborn child. I felt responsible for their well-being and, given that my line of work could not provide for them, I couldn't let this golden opportunity just disappear.

" 'Wait,' I said to the old man as he was about to step out. 'What is it you require from me?'

"The visitor stepped back inside and a soft, sinister laugh escaped from his lips as he turned round and handed me the envelope. His instructions were simple enough, if odd. I was to ask for the assistance of a Mr Sherlock Holmes upon the mystery of the wooden diamond's appearance at my house. I was also to convince you and Dr Watson to come and visit my shop and investigate the case. The whole affair had already unnerved me considerably, both with the old man's appearance as well as his unusual request. It is not to be marvelled at therefore that I felt I would go mad when my fabricated story actually turned out to be true and I found myself facing the wooden diamond on my front door. I could not comprehend how that very same object could have made its way to my house when I had placed the box with its supposed contents on the shelf after I left your lodgings in Baker Street."

He spoke with an exhausted and resigned voice. Yet, a peace reigned in his eyes as he looked at both of us. A peace which is only brought about when one professes the truth to others and exposes a long-held lie.

"Ah! That may have been a little trick on my part," proclaimed Holmes who had remained quiet throughout Eldridge's account. Now, full of energy he explained to us all how he came to see beyond the veil of trickery.

"I find that the most effective way to lure a dishonest individual is to make them think that their dishonesty was not completely unfounded. The reaction to a seemingly impossible occurrence is enough to bring forth the guilty party.

"I suspected something was amiss as soon as you spoke of the discovery of the wooden diamond at your house. Clearly, only you had access to the shop and the box in which it was found. Whilst anyone could break in and steal the frame, it was impossible for them to have brought it here to your front door before you yourself arrived home, unless they had taken a cab. But then again, to what purpose? The mystery of the old man's request and his failure to pick up the work he commissioned did not make sense. I soon suspected some trickery in the story itself which could only be resolved by a revealing response from the storyteller himself. I therefore devised a scenario whereby Watson would give you a short tour of my experiments in the kitchen, which allowed me to replace the wooden diamond with an equally heavy object in the box. This would give you the impression that you had taken the contents you came with back to the shop, whilst in truth I had retained the object myself.

"Concealed within a rather large coat, I made my way here to Woburn Place and hung the frame on your front door. I meant to play with your disbelief by making you think that the wooden diamond had remained locked in your shop. If your story was true, another occurrence of this incident would not have resulted in such outlandish behaviour. Your actual reaction, however, proved the contrary. With the trap set, I could only wait for the revelation. Meanwhile, the visit to your shop helped to further substantiate any unresolved issues.

"There I was able to confirm that the box had only moved twice ever since you placed the diamond inside upon its completion. You had remarked that the top shelf is about six feet in height. You yourself, Mr Eldridge, are just over five feet. In order to show the result to the old man, you had to slide the box outward before taking it off the shelf. The same thing happened before you brought the package to our lodgings. There were two distinct lines of recently deposited dust particles on the floor just under the shelf. In addition, the shelf itself exhibited a clear square patch where the box had been placed. There was another set of lines of dust which had accumulated at the back of the shelf when you pushed the heavy box back on top. That is the singular gift of a dusty shop. One can easily infer where and how many times an object has been moved by a simple analysis of the patterns formed by the particles. That particular shelf was coated in a fine layer of undisturbed dust, except where the box occupied the space. The clues were easy enough to reason with. You had clearly moved the box only twice and those have been accounted for. Therefore, any claim that the object had somehow made its way off the shelf any other time was unfounded.

"There was also the other issue of the ink drops. A quick examination of your writing area revealed the dip pen you used to write the note. There were two distinct ink drops at the edge of the counter. Their shape was cut in half, which meant that the other half of the drops fell somewhere else. Yet, there were no such ink marks on the ground like the ones you currently have on your trousers. The two drops had fallen on the surface of the table and onto the writer.

"There was no more conclusive evidence that needed to be unearthed and so we proceeded to come here and lay the trap."

Thomas Eldridge sat in a stupor as my friend explained the whole chain of reasoning which led him to the conclusion of this incident.

"Having taken the case and successfully brought me to your shop, what was next in the plan?" inquired Holmes, who had now leaned forward in his chair and stared intently at Eldridge.

"I don't know. I was simply to get you to take the case and see the note," he replied.

"Then I was right in thinking that it was intended for me," remarked Holmes.

Thomas Eldridge lowered his head and nodded in agreement. His wife looked at him through her tears, but she clasped his hands all the more firmly after his confession.

Holmes leaned back in his chair, closed his eyes and sat in silence. The subtle smile, which had formed on his face at the revelation of the note's intended recipient, quickly faded into a stern frown.

Suddenly, Thomas Eldridge rose from the chair and his wife stood up next to him still clutching his hand. He spoke quietly, but with resolute determination. "So what now, Mr Holmes? I have done you an injustice with my false claims and undoubtedly committed an improper act in the eyes of the law. I am ready to pay for that error."

There was a moment of awkward silence. Holmes looked intently upon Eldridge, who stood with his arm round his wife, whilst their daughter came in and remained partially-concealed behind her parents. My friend's expression was cold and unflinching, as if he was about to proclaim a terrible judgement.

"Good night Mr Eldridge," he suddenly announced, as he rose and made his way out of the front door. "I do hope we never hear your footsteps at 221B Baker Street in the future," he added. I stood in that house, confused at the turn of events that had just occurred. Looking back and forth between my departing companion and the astonished faces of the Eldridge family, I finally ran out of the house.

We took no cab that evening, but instead walked steadily along the gas-lit streets of London. Holmes was silent, and I ventured no words as I understood the intense emotions he was experiencing, all concealed behind an unshakeable stern expression. Even the great calculating machine behind Sherlock Holmes could occasionally find itself at the mercy of human emotion.

Perhaps it was the banality of the case itself. Perhaps, touched by the predicament of an expectant wife and helpless daughter, the indomitable spirit of London's finest consulting detective had been rattled by the exasperated measures undertaken by Thomas Eldridge for the sake of his family.

It was not the first time that Holmes had allowed a case to remain hidden from the eyes of the law, and this particular incident was destined to the same fate.

"Well, this case certainly hasn't fulfilled your expectations I see," I remarked as we found ourselves back at our lodgings. Sherlock Holmes had sat down in his armchair with his eyes closed and hands together. I sat opposite him, wondering what he was thinking.

"You have misdiagnosed my disappointment, my dear Watson," he replied after a while. Opening his eyes, he reached for his clay pipe and bag of tobacco, filled the pipe, lit the contents and sent a cloud of smoke high up towards the ceiling.

"The case, while a most trifling affair in itself, has presented a most intriguing feature of interest."

I leaned forward, eagerly awaiting my companion's thoughts.

"The mystery of the old man with the bent back," he continued. "It is rather obvious that the man's disguise and the setting up of Mr Eldridge's story was merely done to attract my attention." He inhaled the burning tobacco and puffed out another cloud of smoke.

"A disguise?" I ventured to ask, after some moments of silence. "You think the old man's appearance was nothing more than trickery?"

Holmes shifted in his chair and extracted the pipe from his mouth. "Clearly. Whilst the case of Mr Eldridge's mysterious wooden diamond has been seen through to the end, there is another, more complex and, dare I say, dangerous case ahead of us."

I looked at my companion as he gazed deeply into the darkening evening outside the window. Suddenly, he turned round and rose sharply from his chair. Abandoning his pipe on the mantlepiece, he dashed towards the kitchen. The contents of the flask, which had been boiling over a flame since morning, had assumed a green tint.

"And now, Watson, I believe my experiment is close to completion," proclaimed Sherlock Holmes as he sat down at the table. Leaning forward, he began pouring out the contents into a small test tube.

He would say no other word that evening and stayed up late in the night conducting his research. As for the mystery of the old man, my friend would not pick up the trails of that most singular case until much later and in dire situations.

The Noxious Intruder

Sherlock Holmes' reputation bloomed considerably in the spring of 1888 as an unstoppable wave of clients, desperately seeking advice and assistance from my companion's extraordinary skills, made their way to 221B. One morning, having just finished my breakfast, Holmes burst into our kitchen in his dressing-gown, holding up a newspaper in front of me.

The large heading read:

Mystery solver strikes again

"I do wish you wouldn't sensationalise my cases, Watson," he said with a sigh. Holmes reached out for his clay pipe and lit the contents. A remnant of unburnt tobacco, which had lain in the charred bowl since the night before, went up in a puff of smoke.

"I write what I see and experience. Nothing which I publish is in any way unassociated with the truth," said I with some frustration. Noting down Sherlock Holmes' methods and our adventures together was a pleasurable and gratifying pastime, and my companion's abrupt remarks towards my work were never to my liking.

"Clearly the public have acquired a keen appetite for your stories. Not least our latest case which you have compiled under the title of *The Adventure of the Blank Photograph*," replied Holmes, as he refilled his pipe and filled the air with a fresh cloud of smoke.

"You must admit, Holmes, that the extreme circumstances of that problem, and your exceptional deductive skills, helped popularise the singular incident of Miss Dillenberger's story," I challenged, as I rose from the kitchen table and followed my friend into the sitting-room.

"I'd rather you focus on the analytical process of my methods than the human side of it, just the same," he shrugged, seating himself in his armchair. His eyes lay fixed on the open window as the distant bustling noises from outside echoed through into our lodgings. The active nature of this great city had long been roused that morning and would not cease until the evening had deepened and brought with it the tranquil silence of human slumber. For the moment, the bright sunlight of a beautiful Saturday morning in May pierced through the thin veil of the curtain and fell upon my companion's stark features. Having sternly waved off my comments on my writing, his mind drifted off into a distant realm, one focused on putting to work again those exceptional skills for which individuals from all over Europe sought his assistance.

A few moments of silence had passed since I sat down opposite my companion; silence accompanied by occasional puffs at his pipe. I watched his composed posture and intense stare towards the street. The bustling noise outside gradually grew louder until a series of irregular thumps disturbed the stillness in our room. Two men came rushing in abreast through the door, pushing each other, until one of them triumphantly squeezed through the entrance before the other and stood inside our sitting-room.

They wore dark overcoats and each had just removed his much battered and weather-stained hat. One of our visitors had the recognisable ferret-faced features I had remarked on in previous cases, whilst the other was paler with flaxen hair and a slight hunch in his back. The two stood breathless next to each other looking expectantly at my companion, whose face remained fixed on that busy world outside the window.

"To what do I owe the pleasure Messrs Gregson and Lestrade?" remarked my friend after some time. The men displayed confused expressions at being identified merely by the sound of their footsteps, but they seemed to think better than to ask for yet another deductive explanation from their esteemed consultant.

Gregson opened his mouth to speak.

"It's a new case," blurted out Lestrade, looking cheekily at his frustrated companion.

"One of those puzzling cases that tickle your fancy, Mr Holmes," put in Gregson. He turned on the other Scotland Yard inspector and smirked in return.

I watched the two men as they battled against each other for my friend's attention, but Holmes sat motionless without turning his head round.

"What are the details?" asked my companion.

The inspectors remained silent and their faces turned into a frown. Now that each had paused to let the other speak, neither seemed willing to answer the question before the other ventured to talk.

"We have none so far," said Gregson with some difficulty.

"At least nothing specific," added Lestrade, who took a step forward into the sitting-room. His colleague followed suit.

"Well? A murder? A theft? A distress call? Surely you must have some information for having come all the way here to seek my assistance," puffed Holmes, as the cloud of smoke grew larger around him.

"We're not exactly sure Mr Holmes," replied Lestrade timidly. "We were sent a telegram early this morning from a Miss Ruthford, seeking immediate assistance at Morsley Manor in Kent."

"I decided to escort Inspector Lestrade on his journey and investigate the problem at hand," interjected Gregson. He took another step forward and now stood further ahead than his colleague.

Lestrade looked frustrated at the abrupt interruption and eyed Gregson's movements with intense scrutiny. Having regained some composure, Lestrade continued his account.

"This morning we took the 6:45 train to Dartford Station, and after a ten-minute drive by hansom, we arrived at the town outskirts to behold the red brick structure of Morsley Manor surrounded by a lush land thick with elm trees. We knocked at the door and were shown in and introduced to Miss Ruthford, the housekeeper.

"Her composure was shackled and a nervous disposition seemed to have taken hold of her. Mr Stanbury, a man of some noble repute and to whose family the Manor has belonged for generations, is her master. Together with Mrs Stanbury, they have lived a tranquil life until the evening before we received the telegram. Miss Ruthford was in a state of confusion and distress as she recounted how her master had walked into his study before going to bed, and how he had not yet emerged. The room was locked from the inside and no other key was available. Together with the groundsman, Miss Ruthford's attempts at knocking yielded no reply. Fearing that some stroke of misfortune had befallen her husband, Mrs Stanbury plunged into a state of utter despair and was taken to recover in the couple's bedroom.

"Mr Stanbury's study had a large window which looked over the grounds behind the Manor, but it was impossible to seek any entrance from there, or look inside to discover what had occurred, for the room lies one storey above the ground without any possibility of scaling the wall. In her distress, Miss Ruthford sent us the urgent telegram seeking assistance."

"I instantly reassured her that the finest of Scotland Yard's detectives would see to it," remarked Gregson, with a gleeful smile on his face.

"Yes, and that is what we have precisely done so far," said Lestrade, clearing his throat.

Sherlock Holmes had maintained his stationary position throughout the account but subtly shifted his head to one side. "Well, what of Mr Stanbury's predicament? Surely two strong men like you could knock a wooden door down," he remarked, with a sarcastic ring to his voice. The plumes of smoke had by now enveloped his whole frame and threatened to pervade the entire room.

The Scotland Yard's detectives were rather taken aback by my companion's remarks. They looked at each other with some awkwardness before Lestrade moved forward and produced a piece of paper from inside his waistcoat.

"Before attempting to force their way into the room, both Miss Ruthford and the groundsman found this note wedged underneath the door."

Holmes remained silent and made no attempt to accept the paper being presented to him. Grumbling, Lestrade opened it and read aloud:

let Sherlock Holmes be the first to bear witness

The sound of those words, both concise and ominous, trailed off and mingled with the bustling noise outside. I looked at Holmes and noticed him placing the clay pipe, still emitting wisps of smoke, on the small table next to his armchair. Snatching the note from Lestrade, he examined it carefully. The piece he held seemed more like a fragment torn from a sheet of paper, with the handwriting ragged and unsophisticated.

Lestrade took a few steps back and rejoined his colleague. Gently, Holmes rose and took a step towards the window, slamming it shut. Almost like a sophisticated dance, he turned round to look at the inspectors. His face was clearly showing an unmistakable suppression of joy which, having been accustomed to my friend's characteristics for years, he was attempting to shield from the expectant Gregson and Lestrade.

He crossed the room. "Watson, your coat and hat. And not a moment to lose!"

He dashed past me and in between the two inspectors, straight out of the door.

Soon, the four of us, found ourselves on the 11:30 train to Dartford Station on our way to Morsley Manor.

Just before one o'clock, we alighted from the cab we had taken from the station, and walked up towards the red-bricked structure. It was evident from the weathered colour of the brick that the passing of time lay heavily on the building, but it nonetheless evoked a sense of history and pride. The Manor itself was a two-storey, rectangular building enclosed by a wall of grey granite running around the grounds, with a metal gate from which a path led to the front door. Several windows adorned the façade of the building and a few wisps of smoke emerged from the blackened clay chimneys on the roof.

The path that we now walked on was a narrow gravel road leading up to the gate. It was flanked on either side by a heavily-wooded area of elm trees, within which a thick layer of fog had risen to cover the surrounding grounds of the Manor. The air had turned damp as we approached Dartford and, by the time we walked up to the gate, our garments were covered with fine droplets of moisture.

Lestrade and Gregson had overtaken us along the path towards the front door. Each seemed determined to arrive at the Manor before the other. At the entrance stood a policeman who had been dispatched to stand guard and report any new developments to the inspectors. He was briefly questioned by our companions and, after an indistinguishable answer from the constable, they headed inside. Next to me, Holmes maintained his characteristic composure and sternness, as he looked up at the façade and its many windows. His mind was clearly absorbed by the case, and had been so since we boarded the train. He had said no word, but had stared incessantly out of the carriage window towards the scenery outside. I had no doubt that despite his absorbed expression, he was not admiring the beautiful countryside through which we were travelling. Rather, he pondered every fragment of the scarce information that had been communicated to him that morning by the Scotland Yard inspectors.

Now, he paused on the doorstep. His stern countenance gave way to a slight smile as he looked towards me.

"Let us unravel this mystery."

He reached the door and headed inside, with me following behind. We found ourselves within a long corridor exquisitely furnished and lavished with several framed paintings hanging on both walls. At the far end, the two inspectors were approached by an attractive woman, not more than forty years of age. Her pale face spoke of recent distress, and her trembling frame evidenced the strange occurrence in that house.

Lestrade greeted her and removed his hat. Gregson followed his colleague's gesture.

"Miss Ruthford, we have come to seek an end to this mystery and remove the cause of your predicament and that of your mistress," offered Lestrade.

Gregson inched his way forward and stood next to the other inspector, offering a comforting smile. "We have brought the esteemed Mr Sherlock Holmes with us, to whom the note was intended." He gestured a hand at my friend, who in turn stepped forward and presented himself to the housekeeper.

"Oh good sir! Thank you for coming here." She pushed her way past the inspectors and grabbed hold of Holmes' right arm with much intensity and vigour.

"Miss Ruthford, may you kindly take us to Mr Stanbury's study?" Sherlock Holmes' demeanour was the finest example of calmness, concealing an intense interest in pursuing the matter before him. "But before we do, may I kindly borrow a fork and your smallest available teaspoon?"

His odd request having been obliged, the four of us followed Miss Ruthford down the corridor and ascended a winding staircase which led us into another long corridor richly decorated with fine carved furniture and exquisite wallpaper. Towards the farther end stood a rough-looking man, with a weather-beaten face and worn attire. He leaned against the wall next to a dark polished door. Its surface glistened in the bleak light coming from the window panes that stood at the north and south ends of the corridor.

"Blazes!" he said in a rough voice as he saw us approaching. "As sure as anything, nothing's stirred in there since this morning ma'am." He pointed at the door and then coughed, making an odious gurgling noise in his throat.

"Thank you Mr Barker, these gentlemen will take over now," uttered Miss Ruthford with a weak smile.

The man gave a slight nod and, raising himself from the wall, he walked passed us with an inquisitive stare whilst mumbling inaudibly.

"Mr Barker is the groundsman of the Manor," attested Miss Ruthford, as if in reply to my intrigued expression.

In the meantime, Gregson and Lestrade had placed themselves in front of the door.

"A moment Inspectors!" Holmes raised his hand sharply, placing it on Gregson's left shoulder. He gently pulled the inspector backwards and stepped forward in front of the door. Extracting his lens from the inside of his coat, he conducted a close examination of the outer frame of the door. He analysed every crack and crevice, the handle and the lock, and finally satisfied himself by a close inspection of the threshold. As soon as he bent down towards the gap between the door and the floor he jerked his head slightly backwards in an impulsive recoil. He sniffed audibly and a bitter expression clouded his face as he stood up and took a step backward.

"It would be wise to circulate some fresh air before proceeding inside," he announced, looking at the inspectors and gesturing towards the corridor windows. In response, the officials looked at each other with questioning glances. "Perhaps now would be a good time to act sirs," he added with a distinct tone of frustration in his voice.

"You too Doctor," he said looking at me in turn, "make sure none present here find themselves experiencing any unwanted symptoms."

"Symptoms, Holmes? What symptoms?" His last statement had completely confounded me, amid his already strange behaviour that morning. He placed his finger onto his lips, which conveyed absolute silence from me and everyone in the corridor.

Gregson and Lestrade joined us once again, as a fresh and chilly country breeze drifted inside from the north-facing window, closest to Mr Stanbury's study. Holmes moved cautiously forward towards the door and stretched both hands outwards.

"As cold as this refreshing air is, I must ask you to move back and not interfere with the contents of the room once the door is open," he proclaimed.

We all silently complied as we took a few steps back from Holmes' motionless figure. Not until we had cleared the space by a few yards did he step closer to the door. Extracting the fork and teaspoon he had borrowed moments earlier, he knelt in front of the escutcheon keyhole decorated with an intricate floral design of symmetrical lilies. The same embossed device was to be found on the front gate and represented the heraldic emblem of the Stanburys, a motif which adorned much of the Morsley Manor interior and exterior.

Poking both kitchen utensils through the keyhole, he twisted the teaspoon gently whilst pushing the fork further inside. There appeared to be the sound of a key falling with a small thud to the floor. After a few seconds of careful adjustments, the lock clicked and Holmes gave a sharp pull at the tools, placing them back into his pocket. Standing up, he stepped backward, placed his hand on the handle, took a deep breath, and opened the door.

Sherlock Holmes' imposing stature stood in the doorway outlined by weak rays of light that filtered through a large window at the other end of the room. His well-built frame concealed most of what lay within, but from where I stood I could clearly see the disorganised state of the study. Large amounts of papers were strewn across the carpeted floor around what looked like a small writing desk. My friend remained motionless on the threshold for less than a minute, before he walked inside and made for the window.

The true horror of the scene was suddenly revealed to us all. There lay the twisted body of Richard Stanbury, lying slumped on a chair with a wide-eyed expression and open mouth; it was an expression sculpted in extreme agony and fear. A single, horrifying moment in time was branded on his face, the circumstances of which could barely be guessed at. As all of us stood frozen in the corridor, looking at the hapless body of Mr Stanbury, Holmes, having successfully opened the window and glanced briefly around the room, emerged with a quickened step and a detectable flush on his cheeks.

A ghastly smell emerged from the study, stifling and foul. Fortunately, the cool air from the window blew away the strong reek that pervaded in and around the room entrance.

"I would not venture inside for the time being." As he spoke, Holmes' breathing was deep and agitated. Walking towards the corridor window, he inhaled and exhaled for a few moments. His behaviour went unnoticed by both Gregson and Lestrade, as well as the others, who had kept their eyes fixed on the brutal scene before them.

Miss Ruthford's face had turned deathly white. Her eyes rolled uncontrollably for a moment, before Mr Barker – whose trembling frame was enough to demonstrate his shock – extended both arms to stop her from falling to the floor.

I looked back at Mr Stanbury's body. The sheer oddity of its posture, the state of the room and my friend's unusual behaviour, made that scene even more impressionable. A chill ran through my body as the cold air rushed steadily rushed into the study. Try as I could, I found myself looking at the dead eyes and gaping mouth. Suddenly, a piercing scream seemed to lunge at us from the corpse, which almost sent me into a whirlwind of confusion and panic. A cold sweat enveloped me when I turned round to find Mrs Stanbury's stunned expression at her husband's death. Dashing towards her, I seized her under her arms as she fell in a swoon.

"Inspectors!" I cried with some difficulty. Both Gregson and Lestrade snapped out of their stupor and came to the assistance of Mrs Stanbury.

"Perhaps you would be so kind as to follow Miss Ruthford downstairs," Holmes said to the officers. When Mrs Stanbury's unannounced arrival had shaken us all out of our wits, he had rushed forward from the open window to seek the cause of the disturbance and was now on his way to regain full control of the situation.

Following Miss Ruthford, who still leaned on Mr Barker, Mrs Stanbury was gently escorted downstairs and away from the horror of that room. As they descended, I could better comprehend the sophisticated features of the victim's wife. She was still young, in her thirties, with dark curled hair and a fragility to her that was beautiful.

I turned round somewhat unwillingly to face the scene once again. Holmes had walked back inside the study and was already in a deep state of analysis. His magnifying glass had once again been extracted, and provided a clear view of all the intricate details which my friend had in mind to examine.

From where I stood, I could see Holmes' frame bending over the lower part of the body. With his back towards me, I could not make out what had attracted his attention. He appeared to lean closer, remove something from the victim's attire and place it in his waistcoat pocket.

I ventured inside to take a closer look at the state of the room, which was smaller than I had originally thought. A small wooden cabinet was the only other piece of furniture that could fit inside. This I had bumped into as I walked past the door on the right-hand side. The desk in between the door and the window almost filled the entire space. It was pushed against the left side of the wall, allowing only a small passage on the other side, accessible to anyone who wanted to cross the room. However, barring part of the way was the chair on which Stanbury was slumped.

One thing I had learned from the numerous casualties of war I had supervised, was the indistinguishable fear and pain of death in both young and old. Yet, death had a sinister way of presenting itself, for each lifeless body had its own macabre manifestation to it – the physical features, the mental agitation, the circumstance of the situation. This incident with Stanbury was one of them. Seeing his body lying like that felt both familiar and wholly alien at the same time.

Turning round to face the door from the inside, I spotted the small golden key lying on the carpet where it had fallen when Holmes had unlocked the door. There was no doubt about it. The room had been locked from the inside. He now proceeded with his analysis of a decrepit-looking fireplace behind the desk, close to the window. A layer of dark grey dust coated the bricks surrounding the structure. In the grate lay fragments of unburnt coal which had escaped a fire the previous night. My friend removed the guard and knelt down to examine these particles. He had taken away his lens and was now eyeing the contents of the fireplace with intense scrutiny. I likened his almost rhythmic flow from one detail to the next as a dance, a well-rehearsed set of movements that led Holmes' brilliant mind from one clue to the next.

Seeing my companion busying himself with the fireplace, I approached the body and using my medical background, attempted to diagnose the causes which led to this poor man's death. We had known almost nothing of the Stanburys, and with no knowledge of the man's health, it was difficult to ascertain any conclusive results. However, certain features and characteristics presented themselves to me, making it easier to come to some concrete picture as to the man's final moments.

The skin on his face, which had initially appeared to be pale, was in fact, upon closer inspection, a sickly yellow. His neck and hands also displayed the same type of colouration. Surrounding his dark hazel eyes was a redness typical of a recent fever. Along the lips were smeared a few drops of saliva. The sour smell emanating from the mouth was indicative of persistent vomiting.

"Well Watson? Surely you must have some theory," said my companion's familiar voice. I rose from my close examination of the body to find Holmes with his hands behind his back and with a gleam in his eye.

"As a matter of fact, I have," I replied with some triumph. "Hemolytic anemia. It is the condition of damaged or dying red blood cells in the body."

"The *how* of the crime is rather obvious. The *whom* is sometimes a bit tricky, but never impossible to unveil."

"You know how Mr Stanbury was killed then?" I inquired, without attempting to conceal my astonishment. Holmes noticed this and smiled. The master, having clearly impressed the apprentice with modest work and exertion, relished the superiority of his mind.

"That was evident from the start. What is always difficult to understand is the *why*. Still, the chain of this case is closing fast. The identity of the murderer is the missing link between the *how* and the *why*. Find out the one and uncover the other. Nothing which a few more inquiries won't throw light on."

I followed Holmes down the stairs to rejoin the others. On our way we were met by the curiously satisfied faces of Gregson and Lestrade.

"A rather nasty business Mr Holmes," exclaimed Gregson, as he paused in front of us. "In all my years of service, nothing shook me so dreadfully. Right to the bone it went, and I'm not ashamed to say it."

"Nasty and tricky no doubt, but we've seen it through to the end," remarked Lestrade with a smile, as he stood next to the other.

Looking over at my companion, I could see from his vacant expression that the statements of the inspectors had failed to impress him. On the contrary. An audible sigh of frustration had emerged through his lips following Lestrade's optimistic proclamation.

"Is it so Inspectors? Tell me, how did you solve the case without having even consulted the scene of the murder?" he enquired. Holmes, still with his hands behind his back, became increasingly fidgety during the inspectors' replies.

"Ah, you have your own methods Mr Holmes and we have ours," remarked Gregson. "While you were examining the room's decor, we conducted a thorough investigation by questioning the household occupants."

"Really now? And what conclusion have you and Lestrade come to, pray?" replied Holmes with rising tenseness in his voice.

Lestrade cleared his throat in preparation for his statement. "Given the good repute of Mr Stanbury and the impossibility of conducting a murder in a locked room two storeys high, the conclusion is inevitable. The victim committed suicide."

"Splendid! But before closing the official report, allow me to conduct a few investigations of my own first," responded Holmes, as he brushed past the two and proceeded down the corridor.

"We've done all the necessary questioning Mr Holmes. Anything you'd like to know you can learn from us," said Gregson, amid heavy breathing as he tried to keep up with the brisk pace of my companion.

Holmes stopped beside an open door at the far end of the corridor and turned round, looking suspiciously at the two Scotland Yard officials. "Indeed? Nevertheless, I should like my own version of the facts." With that, he walked through the door and the rest of us followed him into the Manor's parlour, leaving the inspectors rather annoyed.

"I do hope you're feeling better Miss Ruthford," said Holmes as he approached the housekeeper, who was sitting in an armchair. The colour had returned to her face and her weak disposition was gradually regaining strength. "I would like to ask you some further questions about Mr Stanbury."

"Blazes!" cried Mr Barker the groundsman, as he stood with crossed legs leaning against a bookcase, scowling at my friend.

"Mr Barker, perhaps you could enlighten us on the present situation." Holmes left Miss Ruthford's presence and walked towards the man. "I have noticed, upon coming here, the rather disgraceful state of the Manor's grounds. Are you quite the appropriate groundsman for Morsley Manor?"

A gurgling sound escaped from Barker's mouth. His face was contorted with anger, as he pushed himself away from the bookcase and threw a hard punch. Holmes, who on many occasions demonstrated his skill in the art of fisticuffs, made no attempt to defend himself or deflect the blow which fell hard onto his left cheek. He staggered backwards as I rushed forward to keep him on his feet, whilst Gregson and Lestrade restrained the groundsman.

Examining my friend, I noticed a red rash had already formed on his cheek but there was no bleeding. Worried for his safety, I asked him several times about his welfare. He only looked at me and smiled.

"Well, that was rather conclusive," he said with some difficulty, as he stood back up on his feet. "Thank you Mr Barker for your assistance."

He turned round towards Miss Ruthford and Mrs Stanbury, who had headed towards each other in consolation, following the preceding incident.

"Mrs Stanbury, as difficult as the time may be, I kindly need to ask you a few questions," said Holmes, assuming his distinct and calming demeanour. The widow looked away, as she clutched at her housekeeper's arms. The paleness had returned to her face. I looked upon her with pity, unable to comprehend the awful situation she was forced to come to terms with. Her husband lay dead upstairs, her world was shattered and her future bleak.

"I'll answer for Mrs Stanbury if I may," replied the housekeeper, looking in earnest towards her distressed mistress, "and perhaps she may correct me if I find myself drifting away from the truth."

Mrs Stanbury gave a weak nod and Miss Ruthford obliged.

"What can you tell me about Mr Stanbury and his position as master of Morsley Manor?" asked Holmes.

Miss Ruthford looked once more at her mistress and then began her account.

"I've been employed here for over ten years now. Mr Stanbury had very graciously accepted me in the position of housekeeper. He was an honest and kind employer who asked nothing more of me than to perform my duties. He was also proud of his ancestry and, as inheritor of the Manor, a worthy descendant of the wealthy families who maintained the Morsley grounds. Together with Mrs Stanbury, the prime example of a caring and dedicated wife, life as a housekeeper was idyllic.

"Mr Stanbury occupied a managing position at the Cox and Co. bank in London. Although money was not a financial issue, he loved to work and keep himself occupied – managing to maintain his position as heir of Morsley Manor whilst excelling in the banking business."

The housekeeper paused a moment and sighed. She looked at her mistress who had remained motionless beside her, before she continued.

"Much of this remained unaffected throughout the years, and it was indeed these past two months that a considerable change occurred. Mr Stanbury had a reputation of being a punctual man, both at work and in his private life. He used to leave for London early in the morning and arrive back after six, just in time for dinner. However, his routine then became unpredictable. At times he would come late in the night and without any explanation to his wife as to his tardiness. This I know since Mrs Stanbury grew to confide in me more and more, as she found herself being distanced from her husband.

"Whereas before he always kept his calm and composure even during the most difficult of times, he now flew into fits of sporadic anger for the most trifling of concerns. His appearance too showed signs of change. The few times we ever saw him at the Manor he seemed aged, paler and tired to the point of exhaustion. He went less and less to London, and a growing fear appeared to have crept upon him. His time was spent in his study, locked away all day, and would only show up for supper. Then, one day this routine of his ceased altogether. "

"Pardon my intrusion on your most lucid account, Miss Ruthford," put in Holmes as he took a step forward towards the two women, "but can you confirm if the room we've just been in was not Mr Stanbury's usual study?"

"You are right Mr Holmes. His study was here, just opposite this parlour. One evening he came to me, demanding the key to the small room upstairs. His eyes were wild with fear and apprehension and I dared not go against his orders. Since that time, he has stayed in that room."

"What about food and other supplies, how did he acquire them?" asked Holmes once more.

"Every few days we left some food and other provisions at the door. By the evening they disappeared," replied the housekeeper.

"Thank you for the clarification. Kindly proceed." Holmes rose and took a step backward, placing his hands once again behind his back as he continued to listen to the account.

"There is little much else to say, Mr Holmes. This went on for weeks and the once proud demeanour of Morsley Manor succumbed to the curse that seemed to have invaded us. It was yesterday evening when, having briefly showed up for supper, he locked himself in the upstairs study."

"Did you notice anything out of the ordinary about your master?" asked my friend.

"Well, as a matter of fact, he looked even more ill than usual, as if a malady had taken hold of him. Mrs Stanbury implored him to speak about his predicament, but her tears were wasted. He only stared with vacant eyes at the plate in front of him, from which he ate nothing. Leaving the table without a word, we heard his footsteps ascend the staircase and realised he had locked himself in the room. The next time we saw him was this morning ..."

Miss Ruthford collapsed into a sob as she came to the end of her account. Her mistress had joined her in her lament.

"Thank you for your time and patience, ladies. I shall endeavour to seek a successful outcome in these most dire circumstances." Having said this, Holmes surprised me by what he did next. He knelt before the two women and kissed each one on the hand, before standing back up and bowing to them.

In my several accounts, I have remarked the gentlemanly qualities my friend possessed, but this was unlike anything I had experienced during our time together. Holmes had a way of wooing individuals, but such natural courtesy towards the fairer sex was surprising. I could see by the expressions on Gregson's and Lestrade's faces that even they had thought Holmes' actions too chivalrous for his character.

Without a word, Holmes looked at us and then walked out. Before heading for the front door, he peeped inside Mr Stanbury's original study. This was richly decorated and substantially larger than the one in which he had met his fate. After a brief examination of the surroundings, the inspectors and myself followed Holmes out into the foggy and damp road towards the station.

We had left the bucolic life of the country and, by half past four that afternoon, made our way back to the bustling streets of

London. Gregson and Lestrade returned to Scotland Yard, having remained unconvinced by Holmes' more elaborate and unnecessary investigation into what appeared to be a clear suicide. My friend, with his implacable confidence, nevertheless asked for their presence at our lodgings the following morning. If all went according to his designs, the case would be complete by then.

In the meantime, Holmes and I headed straight to Charing Cross Road to meet with Mr Stanbury's employees at the Cox and Co. bank. Among several workers of that esteemed institution, we were to meet the supervising manager.

As we waited in the lobby, in walked a man who must have been no more than forty, dark-haired and a keen glance in his eyes. His tall frame was a match for Holmes as he stepped forward to present himself with a handshake.

"Do I have the pleasure of addressing Mr Holmes?" He spoke in a gentle, almost cautious tone as if his query would be received with stern animosity.

"Indeed, sir." Sherlock Holmes extended his hand in greeting.

"My name is Michael Scrawley. I have overseen Richard's work ever since he started his employment with us." He paused for a moment and sighed. "Terrible, absolutely terrible," he said with some difficulty. His eyes drifted vaguely for a moment, as if recollecting his friend's face. It was evident that the man was of strong character, highly educated and fluent with the spoken word, as he mastered his anguish and maintained a measure of composure. He spoke with a soft and clear voice. "What a tragedy! I hope I can be of assistance in any way." His demeanour was calm as he recounted the recent oddities manifested by his colleague.

"Richard was an excellent employee – hard-working, efficient and a decent human being." He paused for a moment as his expression turned into bitterness.

"Lately, however, he displayed an unusual attitude. It started with him showing up late and looking exhausted. This persisted until he failed to show up completely. I was, perhaps, his closest friend here, but try as I might to understand his predicament, I failed to shed much light on the situation. He did confess to me, however, his recent discovery of a gambling club in Northumberland Street, just off the Strand. He never told me, but I guessed he had run into some debt and a fear grew in him of being pursued by some creditors. He didn't have to tell me this as it was confirmed a few weeks later, shortly after Richard's complete absence from work.

"A man of unsavoury character walked in here one day. He demanded to see Richard and would not leave until he had personally confronted him. He demanded the money he had won from him at the gambling tables. The man was uncouth and his frustration was manifesting itself throughout the establishment. We value the service to our customers, Mr Holmes. We tried to escort him out of the premises, but he resisted and became aggressive. I finally had to step in and physically push him out of the building with the assistance of my umbrella."

"An umbrella?" Holmes appeared to be curiously struck by the remark.

"Yes, sir. I confess that I am somewhat an ardent admirer of the art of defence." Scrawley lowered his head as he spoke, and shrugged his shoulders.

"Bartitsu?" added my friend.

"That is correct Mr Holmes. I see you are aware of the art yourself. A practitioner too perhaps?" was the reply.

"Nothing more than a rudimentary knowledge in the field," confessed Sherlock Holmes.

Michael Scrawley's eyes seemed to widen at my friend's shared passion for that obscure style of self-defence which I had not yet been privy to. After a moment, he pressed on in concluding his account.

"I made sure that he inflicted no harm on any passersby, but as he staggered further down the street, his distress seemed to increase. It is not in my nature to allow even such a man to remain unaided. Although I did not fully understand the cause of his troubles, and how Richard could possibly be involved, I confronted the man again and offered to administer a special opiate mixture I myself use in times of great anxiety. My assistance was well received and, having cleared his senses, the man was able to offer some information about his association with my friend.

"My suspicions were confirmed. Richard had fallen deep into gambling debts and a handful of individuals were demanding their spoils of victory. The reasons as to his behaviour and absence from work were finally known, and although I made several attempts to visit him at his house, he never presented himself to me. The last time I saw him was over a month ago, and now this tragedy has robbed me of a dear friend."

Mr Scrawley lowered his head again and rested against the wall. He sighed as he tried to fight off his distress.

"Thank you Mr Scrawley, I believe we have taken already too much of your time. I do hope we will come to a satisfying conclusion as to Mr Stanbury's tragic end." Sherlock Holmes bowed and we left the establishment of Cox and Co. and made our way back to Baker Street, weary from our long journey and the intense drama that had greeted us in the morning. Holmes said nothing during our way back, but I could not help notice a satisfied look on his face, and a smile he was unable to conceal. As he had done many times before, his eyes seemed to see far away beyond the physical world and wandered into the realm of solved riddles and exposed mysteries.

The following day, as Gregson and Lestrade joined us in our sitting-room, Holmes assumed that usual posture in his armchair before he delved into the intricacies of a case and revealed the methods behind his great mind.

"I must admit, my good sirs, that the case you brought forward yesterday is of utmost delight."

The two inspectors looked at each other approvingly.

"A locked room mystery is quite a fascinating scenario in its own right. However, the additional riddle of not knowing what lies behind the closed door is even more alluring. Undoubtedly, the most curious feature of interest was the little note seemingly addressed to me found under the door. Since we were not aware of any crime committed, it was useless to try and question the household occupants or learn more about the potential victim before we had assured ourselves as to the contents of the room. From there, we would be better able to analyse the incident at hand, extract the necessary details of the scene, and use that knowledge to manipulate the outcomes of the case to our advantage.

"Upon inspection of Richard Stanbury's study door, no significant features presented themselves in relation to this case. However, a rather pungent smell emerged from underneath the door itself. The odour was strange and quite distinct from usual household smells. You too, Watson, must have smelt it as soon as the door was opened. To avoid any adverse risks to everyone present, I instructed the inspectors to open both corridor windows and thereby ventilate the area.

"Then came the revelation of Mr Stanbury's fate. Evidently the man had suffered a painful death and, by signs around the room, it was clear that he was quite alone when he died. The primary question, therefore, was how he had lost his life within the confines of the room. Suicide was never a possible argument. There were no clues that Stanbury attempted to harm himself; no open wounds or rope marks around his neck. While the state of the body could lead one to think of self-administered poison, the distinct characteristics of his skin were a fine example of prolonged exposure to specific toxic fumes.

"Ultimately, it was the small fireplace by the window that was most intriguing to me. How could a person inflict death at a distance on someone locked in a small room?

"A thorough examination of the fireplace led to the discovery of a few crystal-like fragments dotting the base of the grate among the remnants of coal. The noxious smell, the physical clues on the body, and the distinct features of this substance, yielded only one possible result. Naphthalene."

Holmes paused to light his pipe, as he always did when explaining his methods of deduction.

I had come across the chemical naphthalene during my early medical studies. It came in the shape of white particles and was primarily used in the manufacture of moth balls, which would account for the strong odour pervading the room, but it had not occurred to me the day before that this substance was the same one utilised in Stanbury's study. Yet, the symptoms found on the body were strong indications of its usage. The yellow hue of the skin, the fever, and the recent bout of illness remarked by Miss Ruthford were strong indications.

"Damaged and dying red blood cells would have led to kidney failure and eventually death," continued Holmes, as if he read my mind and added another piece of his analysis to my thoughts.

"There lies the beauty and the genius of this case: a perfectly-timed murder without any interference from the murderer. Naphthalene has a sublimation point of around 75°C. A considerable amount of the substance, dyed black and mixed with the coal in a roaring fireplace, provided the perfect stage for a murder long in the planning. Exposed to the heat, the naphthalene particles would evaporate into gas and consume the entire room; a gradual process that would have left poor Stanbury exposed to the toxic fumes which ultimately led to him falling ill and eventually succumbing to the poison. Yet, inhalation of naphthalene would take longer than a night's stay in a locked room to have any serious health effects. Night after night, as Stanbury returned from work and his gambling gatherings, he would lock himself in his study, light the fire and inadvertently expose himself to the poison. Last night's attempt was the decisive one. The murderer's careful and precise plans were successful, and the culprit's patience rewarded."

I could see Lestrade and Gregson shift uneasily on the sofa. Their furrowed brows were enough to convey both confusion and awe at the facts Holmes was presenting us with.

"All three other household occupants alluded to Mr Stanbury's recent distress and ill-temper. Over the last few weeks it had become a habit of his to lock himself straight into his study. By the data collected from his colleagues at the Bank, Mr Stanbury had become involved in some serious gambling debts and it stands to reason that his fear of being the victim of one of his creditors was not wholly unjustified. As Miss Ruthford pointed out, his original study was much more spacious and with two larger windows overlooking the Morsley Manor grounds.

"Stanbury was exposed and could not reassure himself of his safety from dangerous individuals who had been triumphant at the gambling tables. This was the main reason why he shifted to the smaller room on the second floor. A major victory in the murderer's plans, no doubt. The confined space would allow for the perfect container within which to release the deadly doses of naphthalene.

"Having discovered the method employed by the murderer, it was necessary to move along the chain of reasoning and discover their identity."

"Mr Holmes!" rose a call from downstairs. We all sat silent and looked towards the open door to our sitting-room. Within moments, swift footsteps ascended the staircase followed by a young boy bursting into the room. His scruffy appearance and jovial tone reminded me of that particular introductory incident in *A Study in Scarlet*. Wiggins, head of the Baker Street Irregulars, ran towards Sherlock Holmes and whispered furtive words into his ear. Upon concluding, Holmes smiled and whispered back to the boy, who soon found himself running back out of the room and down the stairs.

It was my turn now to exhibit the same confused expressions of our Scotland Yard companions. Holmes remained silent, boasting his typical triumphant grin. The only noise which invaded the room came from Mrs Hudson's wailing at Wiggins' trespassing. Soon after, Holmes carried on presenting his engaging account of the case.

"Another crucial clue was discovered on Stanbury's left shoe. Lodged in a small crack between the outer and inner sole was yet another piece of paper." Holmes leaned on one side, extracted a torn fragment from his waistcoat pocket and handed it over to me. I opened up the crumbled paper to find the distinctive handwriting from the other message:

to your corpse.

I read out the three words to Lestrade and Gregson, whose confused expressions did nothing but intensify.

"It was blatantly obvious that the message left for me was part of a larger sentence," Holmes proceeded with his account. "The letter *l* of the word *let* demonstrated this fact. If you recall the original note that presumably requested my attention to the case, that piece of paper was torn at both ends. A rather extraordinary slice of coincidence to single out those particular words, but it was evident that the phrase was part of a larger piece."

Holmes had extracted the first note which had originally summoned us to this case. He placed the two pieces together to form a more coherent sentence:

let Sherlock Holmes be the first to bear
witness to your corpse.

"A threat therefore," I stated, leaning forward with curiosity to analyse the two notes on the table.

"Undoubtedly. A single phrase plucked out of a letter from a number which Mr Stanbury had received over the past weeks. Distressed and in fear for his life due to his gambling debt, these letters added fuel to the fire and intensified his anxiety."

"Then the murderer must surely have been one of the creditors pursuing Stanbury," interrupted Lestrade while Gregson nodded his head approvingly.

"There was but one test which would determine the identity of the culprit," said Holmes. "It required a small sacrifice of sorts."

Sherlock Holmes' smile broadened.

"As I'm sure you've all experienced, naphthalene has a particular smell which is difficult to be rid of – especially once in contact with the skin. The murderer would have had to physically conceal the substance and carefully place it with the coal in the fireplace, leaving some residual whiff behind. My face may have suffered the consequences of my little test, as Mr Barker's well-aimed punch flew in my direction, but it was enough to convince me of the absence of the organic compound on his hands, and thus confirm his innocence."

"But where could the murderer have possibly acquired the naphthalene?" I asked.

"It is easily found in the less-respectable corners of the London market business."

The distinct sound of the front door downstairs being opened once again, brought a silence in the study. Holmes had paused from his account and looked fixedly at the open sitting-room door. Both the inspectors and myself followed our companion's gaze and listened to the faint sounds of one or more individuals climbing up the stairs.

"There was but one culprit between the remaining suspects," resumed Holmes, as he kept his eyes on the entrance.

"Kissing a lady's hand may not be a known trait of mine, but is an excellent cover for determining the presence of naphthalene. It ultimately had to be someone who grew concerned about Stanbury's gambling debts, someone who would stand to lose much if he was allowed to pursue his dangerous habits. Isn't that right Mrs Stanbury?"

The composed figure of the victim's wife stood at the entrance. She looked healthier and less frail than the previous night. Her face was visibly perplexed at having found herself in our presence. Wiggins trailed triumphantly behind her. Holmes smiled, rose from his armchair and walked towards the boy. He handed him a guinea and after a pat on the shoulder, the young lad ran off downstairs as Holmes closed the door of the room behind him.

"Now Mrs Stanbury, I do apologise for interrupting your visit to the Cox and Co. bank." He rested against the door as she turned round to face him. "Gregson, Lestrade. Kindly escort Mrs Stanbury to Scotland Yard."

"Holmes!" cried both inspectors, as they rose to their feet in protest. "Have you lost your mind? Mrs Stanbury is the victim's wife," objected Lestrade.

"Surely she has suffered the most and has no need of your foolish tricks," added Gregson.

"She has indeed suffered much, but for far more sinister reasons than you may think."

The woman had grown pale once more as the confrontation between Holmes and the inspectors unfolded. She swayed a little, and then fell down on the sofa. Her breathing was rapid and, as if a heavy weight was being lifted from her, she confessed.

"Quite right Mr Holmes. I loved my husband, but his gambling addiction created a rift in our love. We had lived comfortably ever since we got married, but his habits took a heavy toll on our finances. He was destroying us, I had to stop him."

"Which is why you came to London," added Holmes.

"Yes, to collect any of Richard's money which still remained. I had just alighted in Charing Cross Road when that young boy called me by name and asked me to come here at your request." Mrs Stanbury seemed to have recovered from her affliction as the truth came out.

"And I assume the letters threatening your husband were your doing?" asked my companion.

"Some of them. Others he received were truly from gamblers demanding their money. I had, for some time, been an admirer of your work through Dr Watson's stories. It came into my mind to include you in one of the letters in the hope that it would dissuade him from further gambling exploits. It clearly did not unfold as intended and I was forced to seek alternative means to stop him. Meddling with the packets of coal we left in front of his study assured me that a time would come when the anguish and troubles of my husband would be forever hushed."

A deafening silence followed. I looked at the woman with horror as she calmly recounted her calculating methods to seek the means for a murder. Holmes, with a satisfied expression on his face, finally broke the stillness.

"Thank you Mrs Stanbury. Inspectors," he gestured at the two officials as they stood bewildered after having heard the confession. They escorted the woman out of our lodgings and made their way towards Scotland Yard. From there, her path would lead only to a life in prison, robbed of her husband and money.

"How could love turn into such a bitter state over material gains?" I asked my friend, as we sat back down in our sitting-room opposite each other.

"You are the expert in the field of human emotion, Watson. Surely I cannot answer that question," replied Holmes, relighting his pipe.

"But the note you found under the door and in Stanbury's shoe. How did they end up there?" Whilst the case was solved, there were still details that I had yet to grasp.

"No doubt an extraordinary coincidence brought about by Stanbury having torn the letter and thrown it on the floor. You've seen the small size of that room and the difficulty in manoeuvering yourself around. No doubt the fragments ended up there by Stanbury's frantic pacing."

Holmes' suggestion seemed plausible. In the silence of that room, I could not help but recall the horrid features of the victim and the exceptional circumstances that led to the dreadful revelation of the murderer.

"You know my methods, Watson," said my friend after a while. "I do not rely on coincidences, but I admit that, for the first time, I am thankful for it. For without that single note under the door, I would have been robbed of a singular case, and you of an exceptional story to write."

Sherlock Holmes turned his head round to face the window. He stared intently at the world outside, as he had done the previous day before embarking on the case. Once again, I wondered what that great mind had kept hidden, and whether Holmes looked deeper and further into the case than he had revealed to me.

The Kensington Conundrum

Tragic and foreboding were the newspaper headlines which greeted me one morning in late July of 1888. I found myself alone in our lodgings, having just seated myself at the kitchen table for breakfast. Holmes was out, meandering through the busy streets of London upon some obscure affair. Even as I took hold of one of the newspapers on the table, the black printed letters attracted my attention:

Stanbury Murder: Culprit Dies in Prison

The words struck me both with pity for the woman and a sense of dread, as if a cloud were about to overshadow my future adventures with Sherlock Holmes. Although I realised that I had no cause for such concern, the apprehension I felt was more intuition of something brooding within the criminal world, rather than any physical evidence. The mystery recounted in *The Noxious Intruder* had been solved, the murderer had been identified, found guilty, sentenced, and the case brought to a successful conclusion. Yet, reading the news of Mrs Stanbury's death was unexpected and a sinister motive seemed to be behind this incident.

As I pondered on these thoughts, Sherlock Holmes rushed up the stairs and dashed with vigour into the kitchen. He came in with an air of triumph and threw his overcoat on the empty chair opposite me. In his right hand, he held a note which he placed on the table and pushed forward in my direction.

"Have you heard about Mrs Stanbury's demise?" I asked, ignoring the written message and showing him the newspaper I held in my hand.

"Tragic," replied Holmes. He kept his smile and looked at the note once again. He seemed to avoid my line of questioning and was eager to proceed with the new matter at hand.

"You have read about it then?" I persisted.

Holmes rolled his eyes. He walked round the kitchen table with his hands in his trouser pockets.

"It was certainly expected." I sensed a hint of vagueness in my friend's reply. From where I sat, I could clearly see that his attention was drawn to something else. As he paced to and fro, his eyes wandered up and down as if his mind was deep in thought.

"How could you possibly know this would happen?" I raised my voice and that seemed to do the trick. Holmes snapped out of his dreamy state. He paused and turned his head towards me. He shrugged, walked round to where I was seated, and pushed the note closer towards me, clearly insistent on ignoring my pleas for an answer. "Tut! Tut! That is irrelevant."

"Holmes!"

My friend sighed, visibly irritated by my persistence.

"You seriously underestimate the effects of poison, Watson."

"Poison? What on earth are you talking about?" I protested, my frustration increasing.

"The deed is done. Time to press on, my good Doctor," he replied calmly. Holmes sat down on the chair and, picking the note up from the table, handed it over to me. I stared at him with a stern countenance, for which I received only a smile, while his hand still stretched out in my direction. Seeing no possible way of winning an argument against my esteemed companion, I gave way to this new concern of his. Abandoning the newspaper I had held as evidence during our conversation, I took the note in my hands.

Opening the piece of paper, I read the message that was written on it.

Mr Holmes,
I seek your assistance following a disturbing incident. Will call at 221B Baker Street today at 10:15.
Yours,
Emily Dosett

"That leaves us just five more minutes," said Holmes, checking the time.

"How did you come by this?" said I, rereading the message.

"I was on my way out to Newgate prison when this note arrived." Holmes noticed my questioning glance and smiled.

"Indeed, Watson. I could not resist overlooking such a remarkable turn of events from our previous case without looking into the matter. I had just read about Mrs Stanbury's death and decided to learn more. A few individuals from Scotland Yard would think me more as poking my nose into their affairs." He smiled again.

As the discussion swayed back towards the subject of our initial exchange, I decided to further press my friend into answering the questions that I was desperate to ask.

"Before our client arrives, I would like to know more about the Stanbury case and how you knew she would meet her death."

I have often remarked the sense of frustration that often arose from trying to read the locked mind of Sherlock Holmes. He was ever on guard and avoided saying much of what he knew, preferring instead to withhold information till the very end, before finally revealing it. In the last few months, I noticed a distinct change in Holmes' behaviour. At times, he seemed to fall into a deeper state of thoughtfulness than was usual. His temperament was also quick to flare up. Impossible though it seemed, he took each new case with an even more fervent and rigorous attitude, keeping the facts at hand more and more to himself till the absolute right moment. Whilst I admired my friend for his sense of wisdom and calculated choices, it could be immensely annoying to the expectant listener, waiting for the truth to be revealed.

I remained silent as I began to realise that the strenuous work which he was undertaking had started to take its toll on him. He was never content to let his mind rest, but each case resolved seemed to lie heavily on his mind. He would sit for days on end in his armchair, motionless, staring at the window overlooking Baker Street, but his eyes looked deeper than the physical world before him. Although I could not read his thoughts, I instinctively knew he was pondering on each significant instance that led up to the resolution of each case we had just been a part of. My thoughts went back to the singular circumstances of the mysterious old man in Thomas Eldridge's shop and the whole affair of the Stanburys, which all seemed to point to a single sinister force that had begun to plague a number of our cases. I even recalled those events recounted in *The Hanging Man*, and began to wonder whether that case was in some way associated with this chain of events.

"All in good time Watson," replied Holmes, as if he had just read my thoughts and concerns about him. He waved his hand carelessly in my direction. He headed into the sitting-room, collapsing into his armchair with a long, audible sigh. Witnessing his nonchalant attitude, I stood up in protest, determined not to give way anymore. If there was some perpetrated wickedness haunting our every step towards a dangerous end, I had every right to know about it – even though Sherlock Holmes' brilliant mind was already at work on it.

"Holmes, I need to know what is the matter with you and about these hidden clues and half-solved mysteries."

In my determination to exhibit a stern attitude, I realised I had raised my voice somewhat more than I was comfortable with. This clearly did not go unnoticed by my companion, who frowned, closed his eyes, leaned forward and brought his right hand up to cover his face. He remained still without answering. A silence enveloped the room, accompanied only by the deep breaths of my friend. Suddenly, the downstairs bell rang.

"Ah! I believe our next client is here to enlighten us on her plight," exclaimed Holmes, as his head rose from behind his hand. As if by some trickery, his previous countenance had disappeared and now demonstrated a broad grin and a wide-eyed expression. He stood up and walked across the room towards the door.

Mrs Hudson ascended the stairs and ushered in a young woman who was fair-faced and had a confident sense of disposition. Yet, a feeling of anxiety seemed to reside in her keen glance, which overshadowed her sophisticated features.

She walked in with an unsteady step, cupped hands in front of her. The lady's curled hair was partially concealed under a burgundy bonnet, whilst her long, dark green dress flowed as she moved.

"I believe I have the pleasure of addressing Miss Emily Dosett," said Holmes, as he welcomed her and gestured towards the sofa. She nodded and offered a weak smile.

"This is my good friend, Dr Watson, before whom you may speak freely about the woes that seem to be troubling you," added my companion.

The young woman walked over to the sofa and maintained her composure as she gracefully sat down, but it was evident that some affliction of sorts was disturbing her.

"Watson, perhaps a glass of water for the lady?"

Sherlock Holmes had noticed the same attitude in our client's odd behaviour and, as I was about to make my way towards the kitchen, the woman spoke.

"Some brandy will do me just fine, Dr Watson," she said in a soft, firm voice. We both looked at the woman in surprise. Although some sinister incident was evident in her pale features, she sat erect on the sofa conveying a strong sense of character which set her apart from the tenderness which epitomised the fairer sex. She took the glass eagerly in her hands as I handed it to her and sipped frequently whilst she spoke.

"A most baffling affair, Mr Holmes," she asserted. "I am not someone who is easily put off by bizarre events, but I will not deny that speaking about it to you is altogether comforting."

There was a sense of pride in her statement, and she chose her words carefully as if not to disclose any sense of distress caused by the unknown incident she had experienced.

"Pray Miss Dosett, enlighten us on the cause of your anguish," Holmes uttered in his soothing voice. My companion had abandoned the temperamental attitude of a few minutes earlier and had assumed his usual attentive and eager position in his armchair.

Miss Dosett took another sip of brandy and sighed.

"I come to you from the Ashmore family house at Vicarage Gate, just off Kensington High Street. For the past two years I have been employed as the governess to their young son, and life I admit, has been rewarding. I thought it was all a dream when I found myself in the services of such a well-esteemed family as the Ashmores. The house in Kensington is lavish, but homely at the same time. I was welcomed by all the household and felt I finally belonged somewhere.

Dr Hugh Ashmore, a highly experienced medical man, is a respectable individual if somewhat strict in his discipline towards his son. He is a hard-working character and has always been there for his family. His wife, too, is a gentle soul and although less severe than her husband, she is adamant in the matter of her son's proper upbringing and education. I duly obliged and the parents' gratitude for my hard work was recognised. The child, now six years old, is well-behaved and although prone to the occasional mischief that is characteristic at such a young age, is highly intelligent and has a promising future ahead of him.

"I was tasked with providing teaching instruction for the boy until seven o'clock every evening, after which Dr Ashmore would return from work and the family would meet for dinner before retiring to bed. That is all there is to say about myself and my current situation, Mr Holmes. Truly, no governess would have found a more suitable working place to earn a modest income in these turbulent times. Life as a governess with the Ashmores is ordinary, occasionally exhausting and frustrating, at others highly fulfilling, yet that is but part of life itself, is it not?"

"Indeed," answered Holmes, with a curious twinkle in his eyes as he stared at her intently. His response was somewhat sarcastic in tone, but it went unnoticed by Miss Dosett who, having emptied the contents of the glass, inhaled deeply and resumed her account.

"All was going well until yesterday evening. It was not yet half past five when Dr Ashmore returned suddenly from work. I heard his hurried steps rushing into the parlour where his wife was to be found attending to some knitting. I was with the boy in the next room, but could not hear the conversation which ensued between the two. The rain was battering against the windows and made it impossible to understand what was being said. There was a sudden muffled altercation of voices which interrupted the boy's teaching. Without any explanation, Mrs Ashmore came for the boy and the family retired upstairs leaving their dinner untouched. I remained quite speechless and bewildered as to that bizarre occurrence."

"Pardon me Miss Dosett." Holmes raised his right hand and leaned forward. "Where is Dr Ashmore's place of work situated?

"He is currently entrusted with cases of physical injury at St Thomas' Hospital in Lambeth Palace Road, along the Thames," replied our client. Holmes extracted his small notebook and scribbled rapidly on one of the pages, after which he placed it back in his waistcoat pocket and leaned back in his armchair.

"Thank you, kindly continue."

"Later that evening, I went upstairs to my own bedroom. On my way along the dark corridor, I paused in front of Dr and Mrs Ashmore's room. There was absolute silence and no light seemed to emerge from under the door. Likewise, outside the boy's room. A cold chill of some strange foreboding ran down my spine, but I resisted the temptation to investigate further and respect the privacy of the family. I kept my place and headed to my bedroom.

"I am not usually a light sleeper Mr Holmes, but that night I kept waking and thinking about the events of that evening, when suddenly, at around two o'clock in the morning, I heard a loud sound coming from outside my room. I sat up in bed, with a thumping heart and breathing heavily. I could not make out what might have caused such a noise. I waited in the silence that followed, expecting the rush of footsteps from someone enquiring about the clamour. A few minutes must have passed, without any other sound except the constant rush of blood to my head. I could not bear it any longer. The silence was too profound and menacing, so I rose from my bed and walked as lightly as possible out into the corridor. There was nobody to be seen. Then again, I found myself completely in the dark, except this time, a faint light emerged from under Dr and Mrs Ashmore's bedroom door. I cautiously stopped in front of the room and could distinctly hear some movement inside. Suspecting that one of the occupants had emerged and then walked back into the room, perhaps closing the door in the process, I crept back to my room with a lighter heart."

"I commend your bravery Miss Dosett. It is not an easy thing to face the darkness with such courage after the unusual events you experienced."

"I do not fear the physical characteristics of the dark, Mr Holmes. I fear only the darkness in men's minds that drives them to act with wicked hearts towards other fellow human beings."

"That is very wise madam," replied Holmes.

I myself was struck by the comment. What a remarkable woman. Truly remarkable. Occasionally, as she glanced from one of us to the other, I could distinctly recall the same expressiveness and behaviour I saw in *the* woman. Indeed, our client reminded me very much of Miss Adler, who had so brilliantly outwitted London's greatest consulting detective. Confident, steadfast and perceptive; but, nevertheless, human.

Our client paused for a moment, as if to catch her breath.

"Shortly after, as I lay half awake, with my back towards the bedroom door, I seemed to hear a distinct noise, like a creaking sound outside in the corridor. I could not make out clearly what it was for my senses were dulled. I had a feeling of someone approaching, and quite possibly opening the door. Yet, I was too drowsy to turn round and inspect the cause of this sensation. My feeling of being watched seemed to evaporate after a few moments. Nothing else was heard that night and I fell into a deep sleep.

"By the time I woke up early in the morning, I had almost forgotten the events of the previous night. I readied myself for another day of work, but even as I left my room I noticed that something was amiss. The hall was brightening up with the faint sunlight which filtered through the lower end of the corridor. I found that both bedrooms, the one belonging to the Ashmores and the other to the child, were open and unoccupied. It was at that moment that my heart foresaw some terrible event. The nightly noises came back to haunt me and an irrational sense of dread caught hold of me. I discovered the other rooms in the house were empty, with no sign of the family. There were no indications of any disarray which might have been caused by some struggle with an intruder. It was then that it dawned on me that I was truly alone in the house.

"There was a sinister silence that seemed to penetrate from outside. I like to think of myself as being of strong character, Mr Holmes. One who is not so easily put out by the strangeness and oddities that life sometimes throws at us. Yet, wandering aimlessly through the empty rooms and unable to understand how an entire family could simply vanish in the night posed a strain on my mind. I felt fear and a helplessness within me. The more I thought of the bizarre happenings during the previous night, and the more I looked in vain for any sign of the Ashmores, the more my mind sank into a state of hysteria as I was unable to comprehend what unimaginable tragedy had befallen that household.

"What had happened to that poor boy and his kind mother? Why was I not also victim of this obscure act? Where could everyone be? These questions invaded my head. Confused and overwhelmed by this incident, I did not let my anguish and irrationality take hold of me. I sent at once for the police and immediately sought your renowned services in my plight." Miss Dosett concluded her unique account and sighed deeply. She looked at my companion with keen eyes, expecting some immediate resolve to this mystery. Meanwhile, Holmes puffed away at his pipe, whilst eyeing our client from behind the veil of smoke.

"You have done well to call the police first," said Sherlock Holmes after a while. "Until a discovery of sorts is made, there is no reason to believe that any crime has been committed against the Ashmores."

"Truth be told Mr Holmes, I do not place so much confidence in the police," our client stated, with a subtle smile on her face. Holmes burst out laughing, as he swayed back and forth in his armchair.

"You are a very perceptive and, might I say, honest woman," he said, still chuckling at the remark. "I thank you Miss Dosett for bringing to our attention this most exquisite riddle to solve."

Abandoning his pipe on the mantlepiece, Holmes rose from the armchair and left the room. He returned momentarily in the process of putting on his overcoat.

"Miss Dosett, it would be wise for you to stay here and recover your wits, until we have completed a thorough investigation of the house at Vicarage Gate," he said.

"Absolutely not," protested our client. She rose and looked defiantly into my friend's eyes. "I seem to be as much involved in this as the Ashmores and I intend to see it through to the full." Holmes could not conceal the clear sense of admiration that was written on his face, in response to the tenacity of that woman. He said nothing, but lowered his head and smiled softly.

"Watson," he said, turning round to face me, "I should like your assistance too if you are available."

"Certainly," I replied, "this is a most puzzling mystery and I should like to accompany you towards its successful resolution."

"Excellent! I believe we should be in Kensington by the hour, and then we shall attempt to look beyond this shadowy veil of a problem." Sherlock Holmes smiled at both of us and we followed him outside into the busy life of Baker Street to take a cab.

At half past eleven we found ourselves at the eastern end of Vicarage Gate. Two rows of elegant four-storey houses adorned both sides of the road. The whitewashed buildings gleamed in the morning sun. A few pedestrians walked by, past the occasional elm tree that grew over several of the garden walls. The street itself was idyllic, enmeshed in a peaceful serenity. Alighting from the cab, we had seemingly abandoned the chaotic noise of the city, now but a murmur in the distance. We followed Miss Dosett to one of the houses on the north side of Vicarage Gate. As we approached, two police constables accompanied a distinguished figure who was standing next to the front gate. He was tall and wore a dark brown overcoat. His back was turned towards us and his head bowed down. His right arm occasionally jerked in a rhythmic fashion. The man appeared to be scribbling.

Holmes strode ahead of us and called out to the man.

"Hopkins! So good of you to join us."

The young and fresh-faced countenance of Inspector Stanley Hopkins was revealed as he turned round. On my many adventures with Sherlock Holmes, the inspector had proven himself a good detective and an excellent apprentice in the eyes of my companion. His warm greeting was enough to indicate his delight at our presence.

"Mr Holmes, what an absolute pleasure!" he remarked, as he closed his notebook and placed it inside his coat pocket.

"My mind is now at rest, knowing that you are the investigating officer on this case, Hopkins."

I have often remarked how my companion had a way of conveying confidence and easiness in others. The inspector's face, which had lit up in sheer satisfaction at my friend's remark, had now taken on a frowning expression.

"This case is a real tough riddle, Mr Holmes," said Hopkins as he retrieved his notebook and consulted it. "I cannot shine any light on it."

"Pshaw! My good Inspector. Since I just happen to be here, I wouldn't mind lending a hand in resolving this case with your assistance." Sherlock Holmes winked at the inspector, who now quickly turned into his usual jovial self.

The morning air was filled with the scraping noises of our shoes as we walked along the damp, stone-paved path leading up to the front door. From the richly-decorated doorknob and freshly painted walls, it was evident that Dr and Mrs Ashmore had the means with which to maintain their status, and one of the reasons why our client had found the role of governess an ideal and comfortable occupation. The foyer was captivating with its rich Persian carpets, polished wooden staircase and ample light filtering through from several windows overlooking Vicarage Gate. I was astounded at the amount of furniture and framed paintings which decorated the house.

Heading upstairs, with Holmes occasionally surveying the ground before him, we made our way towards the bedrooms. I vividly recall the impression I had as we slowly ascended the central staircase, when we left behind the bright light of the foyer and plunged into an atmosphere of gloom. The hallway we found ourselves in was equally adorned with works of art and the finest quality carpets, but these could only be vaguely glimpsed in the weak light emitted by the two gas lamps hanging from the ceiling. I walked behind Holmes and Miss Dosett, as they followed Hopkins' lead. This was no criminal incident we were investigating. Nor was there any gruesome murder awaiting us in one of the rooms. Yet, a strong sense of foreboding crept into my heart. The house, which at first felt so welcoming, became hostile and disquieting.

"This is the Ashmores' bedroom." Hopkins stopped next to an open door and gestured inside. "Everything has been left in its original position, Mr Holmes."

My companion stepped forward into the room, with his cupped hands behind his back. His frame was slightly bent as his head swayed from one side to the other. The lavishness found in the rest of the house was also present here: the carpets, the elaborate ceiling beams, and the furniture. The large bed was flanked by two small tables and on the opposite wall was a large brick fireplace. To one side of the room was a white-laced vanity cabinet, while directly in front of the door were a pair of the finest colourful silk curtains concealing what appeared to be a broad glass-paned window. The curtains had remained shut, presumably since the evening before, and allowed for a very faint morning light to penetrate.

Sherlock Holmes moved from one part of the room to the other. He had refrained from using his lens and instead relied entirely on direct observation. He paced from the cabinet to the curtains and back to the bed, with its sheets and quilt left lying in disarray. Clearly it had been in use until very recently and then abandoned in this state. Holmes bent down close to the creased pillows, resting his left leg on the mattress. Momentarily, he assumed a routine of sniffing round the richly-carved headboard and occasionally placing his hands on the area where the two occupants were likely to have slept.

"We've conducted a thorough search of the house, but could not find any trace of the occupants," remarked Hopkins, as he scribbled in his notebook whilst observing my friend's intricate and precise performance.

"It was the strangest behaviour I ever saw from the Ashmores," added Miss Dosett with a slight quaver to her voice, as she stood on the threshold next to me.

Holmes returned no answer, but proceeded with his analyses of the curtains. As he drew them aside, a ray of sunlight entered the room. He unlocked the window and then proceeded to an intricate analysis of the handle, the glass and the frame around the window sill. Having successfully completed this process, he then opened the window and looked out.

"Watson, a moment if you please." The silence had been broken by Holmes' soft, yet decisive tone of voice. He was looking outside, but he extended his right hand behind him and gestured to me to come forward. I walked into the room and approached my friend who had been glancing at the garden on the other side of the house which was filled with rhododendron bushes and fir trees. He seemed to be pointing towards something in the distance.

"Would you say the road to Inverness Gardens lies in that direction?" he said quietly. I looked to where he pointed and descried the rows of houses extending away as far as the eye could see. Closer to the back garden, a short paved corner, which seemed to be the end of Vicarage Gate, appeared to emerge from behind the last house neighbouring that of the Ashmores.

I surveyed the area as best I could from that angle and tried to piece together the vague recollections I had of passing through the area which, until that day, had been scarce. However, Holmes' judgement seemed logical.

"Yes, I believe it lies roughly over there." I pointed vaguely in the direction of the road.

"No, it lies *exactly* over there," replied Holmes in a persuasive and confident manner. "Miss Dosett, you said you heard a noise during the night coming from somewhere in the corridor." My friend had moved away from the window and turned round to face the woman still standing on the threshold.

"Yes, Mr Holmes," she affirmed, walking forward.

"And you are positive it was just the one noise?"

"Absolutely. As I said, I could not sleep very well and it struck me as highly distinctive. I heard no other such sound afterwards, except that sense of being watched soon after," she replied.

Holmes chuckled at the answer, as he rubbed his hands together. Clearly, he was onto some scent but, as was always the case, his listeners were as yet left completely in the dark.

"The boy's room is just in here," said Hopkins as he darted towards the door and made his way out into the corridor.

"That won't be necessary Inspector. I have everything I need for the case inside this room." We all looked at Holmes with some incredulity. Were it not for the expression of sheer confidence on his face, I should have thought that my companion was severely restricting the evidence of the case by not observing the state and contents of another victim's bedroom.

Holmes turned round again and headed towards the right corner of the room adjacent to the window. Extracting his lens, he bent down and analysed what looked like a few drops of wax that had fallen on the slightly disarranged carpet. He knelt closer, tracing a clear line of examination which was invisible to the rest of us. He strode back towards the fireplace with the lens still held firmly in front of him, as he knelt down with his face almost against the brick-set hearth itself.

"Halloa, halloa! what have we here?" he remarked. With his back towards us, he seemed to reach out and pick up something from the grate. Standing back up and brushing off fragments of coal dust from his sleeve, I could see his bent frame as he hunched over his discovery, scrutinising it with the aid of his lens.

Miss Dosett, the inspector and myself all stood there, waiting patiently for my friend to reveal his findings to us. We looked at each other after a minute or two had passed but Holmes' figure remained motionless.

"Holmes?" I finally dared to ask, unable to contain my anticipation. There was no reply from my companion. I ventured forward until I came right next to him. He seemed to perceive my movement as he slowly raised his eyes from the object in his hand and stared ahead with that usual intensity which seemed to pierce the physical wall of the room. He spoke no word, nor made any movement.

I looked down to find the lens clutched tightly in his right hand. In his left, between his thumb and forefinger, he held a piece of paper. It looked like the corner torn from some small envelope, but it was difficult to tell from the tiny fragment of evidence that was left. A charred edge showed all that remained following its disposal in the fire.

In the light streaming through the window, I noticed that the piece of paper bore a strange mark. Its intricate design was clear and instantly recognisable. There, between Holmes' blackened fingers, was the unmistakable printed imagery of two small angels: one pointing, the other kneeling in submission.

"Holmes," I whispered, trying to fight off the sense of bewilderment that had suddenly overwhelmed me.

"Yes, Watson, I saw it too," replied the cold voice of Sherlock Holmes. In the silence of that room, his words seemed to echo endlessly. My trepidation at the discovery left me motionless. All those subtle fears which had resided at the back of my mind, ever since we began this series of adventures, suddenly swelled within me. Images of an old man with a soft voice visiting a wood carver's shop in Streatham Street invaded my thoughts.

I looked at Holmes standing still beside me. He assumed that same intense posture and stare that I had seen over and over again whenever some new turn of events took place during our many cases. Yet, this time, there was a hint of change in his expression. Did I detect a flicker of fear in those deep-set eyes? It was uncommon for Sherlock Holmes to evoke any sense of anxiety. Even during some of our most intense cases, he had expressed feelings of concern and uneasiness. He was human after all, and prone to all the strengths and weaknesses of our humble race and at that moment, the very primordial sense of fear was written on his face.

He took a step backward, turned round to face the window and cautiously raised the piece of paper to the sunlight. He used his lens once again to conduct an intricate examination of the printed mark and the texture of the paper itself, until he concluded the session and placed both the fragment and lens in his overcoat pocket.

"Anything of interest, Mr Holmes?" asked the inspector with a questioning glance. Miss Dosett, equally perplexed by my companion's behaviour, took a step forward.

"Please Mr Holmes. Do you have any idea what may have happened to the Ashmores," she implored. Her soft, caring voice seemed to calm both Holmes' and my own nerves. My companion turned to face our client and smiled.

Like the lighting of a candle, Holmes assumed his usual cheeky demeanour. I was always fascinated by his ability to keep his mind off things and not allow other thoughts to distract him from his current chain of reasoning. This he demonstrated so remarkably. He dispelled any fears and questions which had been raised by the discovery of the fragment and plunged back into the case at hand.

"A most singular riddle," he exclaimed, "truly singular." He maintained his typical posture of cupping his hands behind his back and walked to and fro the room as he proceeded with the investigation.

"Let us take the events in order as they have been presented to us. Hugh Ashmore, a man of good reputation and sound medical experience, returns to his quiet household in a state of agitation. We cannot ascertain the cause of his behaviour, but we can take it as a working hypothesis that he was being pursued by individuals upon some matter. Confessing to Mrs Ashmore all about his predicament they send the cook and maid away and make for an early night. A rather odd decision. Why retire to their bedrooms if some pressing danger pursued them? Why not call for the assistance of the police? Clearly this must have been a sensitive matter not intended for any interference from the law."

I looked with strong admiration at Sherlock Holmes, who had now mastered his anxiety following the discovery of the emblem on the piece of paper, and was now back to his usual self in conducting a clear line of reasoning. He kept pacing to and fro in front of us, three expectant individuals.

"Miss Dosett, you remarked upon retiring to your bedroom, that the couple's room was dark and so was that of the child exactly opposite." Our client nodded eagerly, as if expecting some sudden revelation of the mystery.

"Nothing else took place until you heard the loud noise and bravely ventured to investigate it. At that point, a faint light emerged from the Ashmores' bedroom and shortly afterwards, you yourself felt the sensation of being watched as you lay in bed. The disappearance of the entire household except yourself, Miss Dosett, is quite extraordinary."

Holmes paused and looked round the room in which we had been standing. Besides the incident of the fragment in the fireplace, nothing presented itself as out of the ordinary.

"Couldn't they have simply emerged from their rooms and walked out of the front door for some reason?" suggested Inspector Hopkins, breaking the silence. I believe he spoke for both myself and our client. The whole affair seemed rather trivial, were it not for their sudden, inexplicable disappearance.

Holmes sighed and smiled, relishing the opportunity to explain the simplest of deductions which presented themselves as impenetrable riddles in the mind of Scotland Yard officials.

"Never underestimate the importance of a set of footprints my good Hopkins," he stated, "especially those on expensive Persian carpets." He raised his right arm and pointed with his finger to a faint, muddy trail close by the bed and upon the threshold.

"Last night's torrential rain marked Dr Ashmore's hasty arrival after work, and can be glimpsed from the same set of prints at the entrance, up the staircase and leading to this room. I must say I avoided a major catastrophe by noticing the marks upon walking into the house and allowing myself to be the first in this room. There is the slightest hint of two more imprints on the carpet that merge with those of Dr Ashmore from the corridor. Clearly, Mrs Ashmore and their child followed him into this room."

"The boy?" I remarked, looking at the ground in awe as I tried to piece together the images from Holmes' reasoning.

"Clearly. The boy never went into his room last night."

Stanley Hopkins crouched down and looked intently at the dry particles left by the impression of a boot mark close to the bed, barely visible even with the light now shining fiercely into the room. Holmes looked at the inspector's behaviour with a gleam in his eye, before continuing with his assessment.

"I have followed the footsteps carefully and there are no other marks that indicate the occupants left this room through the door. Seeing as the Ashmores are no longer in this room, it is safe to presume that they found an alternative means of escape."

I instinctively gazed at the window, pondering how three people could clamber over the sill and climb down into the back garden. The height was considerable and, with no safe foothold, it seemed to go against the possibility I had conjured up.

"Ah Watson, you begin to question your own doubts at the evidence you see before you. That is good. That distinctive frown, following your initial raising of the eyebrows, says it all. No Doctor, the Ashmores could not have made their way out of the window in complete darkness and with a façade drenched with rain. They clearly left this room by some other route."

"But how is that possible?" I protested, unable to comprehend how my friend was suggesting an alternative which was physically unattainable any other way.

Holmes chuckled.

"It is an old axiom of mine that once you eliminate the impossible, no matter how improbable the supposition may be, it must be true. Perhaps you would all like to participate in my little experiment."

He made his way towards the door and ushered us into the corridor. "Now perhaps, Miss Dosett, you would be so kind as to lock me in the room and make your way with Inspector Hopkins and Dr Watson into your own bedroom. Wait for five minutes inside and then come and unlock this door."

With perplexed faces, we saw that his requests were carried out to the latter. Miss Dosett, unable to hide her frustration at this seeming waste of time, locked Holmes inside the Ashmores' bedroom. We then headed into her room and waited. Time is a remarkable thing to marvel at. Our vigil felt interminably long before the five minutes ticked past and we headed back outside.

Unlocking the bedroom door we walked in.

The scene in front of us left us completely confused. The room was empty and Holmes was nowhere to be seen. The window had remained closed, secured from the inside, whilst the door, accessed only by the key in Miss Dosett's hands, had not been opened. My incredulity soon transformed into fascination at my friend's apparent trick. Suspecting him to have assumed some clever concealment of sorts, we inspected the room inside out. There was no sign of Holmes anywhere.

As we were all engrossed in our investigation, we suddenly froze. There came a faint tapping from downstairs. Someone was knocking on the front door.

We followed Inspector Hopkins out into the corridor and down the staircase. The events that morning had somewhat unnerved our client and myself. Holmes' disappearance just a few moments before had sufficed to convince me that this case was truly unique and more sinister than I had initially admitted to myself. As Hopkins opened the front door we espied the two police constables we had seen upon our arrival.

"Mr Holmes has requested you all to join him," said one of the constables.

"Where on earth is he?" inquired the inspector, with an unmistakable tone of incredulity in his voice.

"Just round the corner, sir. He's in the other street, behind the house." The constable took a step backward and pointed with his hand to the right of the Ashmores' abode. We all walked out and followed the officers round the eastern end of Vicarage Gate, where the path, heading to the east, turned back round to the west and into Inverness Gardens. Were it not for the fact that we had walked there, I would have been convinced that we were in the same street. A new row of whitewashed houses, similar in architecture to the one we had emerged from, ran in a straight line on the opposite side. As we came round into the road, towards our left were the back gardens of the Vicarage Gate inhabitants.

The sun had now risen high and its light reflected off the puddles that dotted the main path of Inverness Gardens. There, in the middle of the road, my eyes fell on the hunched figure of Sherlock Holmes. He was on his knees, with his head almost to the ground. The lens was back in his hand as he crawled along the pavement and towards one of the gardens, presumably the same one belonging to the Ashmores. His overcoat was covered in dust, and every now and then, as he moved, a small cloud of particles would detach itself from his clothing and drift away into the morning breeze. His boots too were much soiled and caked with mud. Upon noticing our arrival, he raised himself up and stood facing us with a most mischievous grin.

"All is well. We need not trouble ourselves with the Ashmores anymore. Indeed, it would be wise to let them be."

He said this with the utmost conviction, which left us in a state of confusion and utter incomprehensibility. Miss Dosett, unable to contain herself any longer, strode forward towards my companion.

"Mr Holmes, it seems I have made a terrible judgement in asking for your services. Clearly you never meant to take my pleas for help with as much dedication as your other cases." Although accompanied by a slight tremor, her voice was steady and confident, the traits of a strong character with admirable resolve.

My companion's smile faded as he looked in earnest upon our client. A reaction showed in his eyes, shifting between pity and care.

"Madam, there has not been a single case of the innumerable I have undertaken that has not received an equal amount of attention. The events presented to us today are admittedly grave and unusual, but I assure you that if you care about the Ashmores you would do well to let the matter rest."

He gave a confident smile and then looked back at the inspector and myself.

"It is evident that the Ashmores made a hasty escape from danger. There are clear marks of a cab driving off." He pointed towards clues on the damp pavement and the cobbled road that lay undetectable to us.

"But how can you be sure that it was the Ashmores who took the cab and not someone else? Good lord, Mr Holmes! And how the deuce did we find you here after having locked you inside the bedroom?" Inspector Hopkins' composure had long fallen, and was instead replaced by sheer astonishment and disbelief, which admittedly also manifested themselves in my own expression.

Holmes chuckled. He placed his hands behind his back and resumed that back and forth pacing that was so synonymous with the great consulting detective enjoying the pleasures of the game.

"It is simplicity itself, my good Inspector. The solution to the one resides in the comprehension of the other." He came over to us and pointed to the Ashmores' house. From where we stood, the bedroom window was visible between two tall fir trees planted in the colourful garden at the back of the house.

"It is highly unusual for an old house not to have some sort of passage to the outside world besides the front door. The impossibility of the Ashmores having disappeared into thin air gave rise to a possible trapdoor somewhere in the room itself. Watson, you may have noticed the drops of wax on the slightly disordered carpet. Having gained some clues, I carried out my experiment. The element of surprise was crucial and therefore I did not disclose any of my thoughts. Once locked inside the room, I removed the carpet and discovered a latch and the distinct outline of a trapdoor in the wooden floor, together with a piece of strong string which can be used to pull the carpet back into position after the trapdoor is closed.

"I went down a long and narrow winding stair until I found myself completely in the darkness. It was then that I missed a candle for my own escape, but soon felt the handle of a door which brought me to a hidden passage leading through the garden shed and across the flowerbed. From then it was elementary. Soiled footprints from where the family had stepped, presented themselves along the garden path until they disappeared abruptly from the pavement, whence a cab had been waiting to take them away."

"What of the noise and the feeling of being watched that Miss Dosett has attested to?" I inquired, feeling overwhelmed by the sudden revelations being presented to us.

"I would say that Miss Dosett has had a very lucky escape in avoiding some undesirable intruders. Clearly their only purpose was to get hold of the family. A sleeping governess, unaware of the private affairs of her employers, was not of interest to them."

"To whom, Mr Holmes?" persisted Miss Dosett.

"Ah! There we come to another riddle entirely. We must be content that no harm befell your employers," replied Sherlock Holmes.

Having concluded his account, Holmes would say no more. He avoided the other questions imposed on him by Inspector Hopkins and bade a skeptical Miss Dosett farewell. I ventured no more myself and our journey back to Baker Street was one dominated by absolute silence. It was clear enough that the discovery of the printed insignia was on my friend's mind and presented a riddle which was far beyond our typical case.

As I alighted from the cab, Holmes remained seated.

"Goodbye Watson. I hope to be back later on this evening," he said. The cab trailed off into the distance, leaving me wondering what line of investigation he was to undertake. Yet, there was no need for me to ask of his whereabouts, for the following morning he confessed he had visited St Thomas' Hospital in Lambeth Palace Road to enquire about Hugh Ashmore. What his results were, however, he would not reveal.

Before writing down the final words of this account, Holmes was quick to rectify my original statement of the case. Although the Ashmore's whereabouts were never discovered, the mystery had been successfully resolved. For Sherlock Holmes, the cause of their sudden predicament and disappearance was another case altogether. He never confessed, but I was adamant that for him, there had been only one case which had been opened several months back and was still in the process of being investigated.

A few weeks had now passed since we received the summons from Miss Emily Dosett on her strange incident. We learned that she had found employment as a governess with another family and, while her position was by no means as rewarding as her previous engagement, she was nonetheless content. One evening Holmes walked into the sitting-room holding a small note in his hand.

"The Kensington case, Watson. Miss Dosett has sent us this note she received recently." Holmes handed it over and made straight for his armchair. In earnest, I took the folded piece of paper and read the message.

Dear Emily,
It is with hope that I send you this brief note. We ruefully regret our sudden departure from such an esteemed friend as you have been. We wish to let you know that we miss you but are unable to meet you again. May these words suffice to reassure you of our wellbeing.
Yours sincerely,
H. Ashmore

I re-read the note, hoping to discover more about the fate of the family. Meanwhile, Holmes had reached for his violin and had begun adjusting the tension of the strings.

"What about that symbol found in the Ashmores' fireplace, has there been no light shed upon it?" I inquired, looking back at my companion who maintained a calm and cool demeanour. His eyes, vacant and distant, looked out through the window while his hands proceeded to place the musical instrument between his shoulder and left cheek.

"Deep waters, Watson, deep waters. Fear not, we shall soon find ourselves upsetting them."

With those foreboding words, he raised his bow and proceeded to play the most exquisite rendition of Antonín Dvořák's Requiem, Symphony No. 8.

The General's Dilemma

Over the months following the somewhat abrupt conclusion to the Kensington case, I detected an unusual reclusiveness in my friend, Sherlock Holmes. He took to carrying out experiments in his own room, which was kept securely locked and inaccessible. This placed a further strain on our friendship following my marriage to Mary Morstan and my departure from Baker Street. In the several instances when I visited our old lodgings at 221B, the lack of new cases being brought forward was exemplified by Holmes' persistence in spending entire days behind closed doors. He would not venture out except for his evening dinner, and whilst he said nothing of his behaviour, I could not help but wonder whether his mind was wholly occupied by the singular discovery of the printed mark on a burnt envelope found at the Ashmore house in Vicarage Gate. A case was the only thing that brought us back to work together, when I was summoned away from my medical practice and my wife in order to join my friend in his singular profession.

It was on a particular morning towards the end of September, 1888 that I received a telegram from Sherlock Holmes himself.

Watson,
New Case. Assistance Required.
2 Days at the most.
– S.H.

Holmes' message was in his typically cold and precise manner. Yet, the summons was a welcome change since my practice had been lacking in patients, and my wife happened to be visiting relatives in the country.

Following a hurried breakfast, I made my way eagerly towards 221B Baker Street where I was greeted by a concerned Mrs Hudson.

"What have we come to?" she moaned, as we ascended the staircase. "Were it not for the almost empty plates I find littering the rooms, one would think nobody lives here anymore." Heading for Holmes' door, she grasped the handle and attempted to push, but it failed to open. Grumbling, she tried again without much success. The door opened a fraction, allowing some light from inside to emerge. I myself attempted to gain access to my friend's lodgings, and after a considerable thrust at the sturdy wooden door we managed to make our way inside. Two large piles of newspapers which seemed to have been stacked behind it had toppled over, clearly outlining the cause of our previous predicament.

"Blast it! Such a horrible mess!" cried Mrs Hudson as she quickly made her way back downstairs. On other days, I would have considered the behaviour of the landlady to be overly theatrical at best. Yet, as I stood in that sitting-room I could hardly agree more with her. Documents, books and all sorts of newspaper cuttings lay strewn across the entire length and breadth of the room. I found myself wading through ankle-deep heaps of paper. It was impossible not to avoid stepping on some headline reporting a political scandal or a neatly handwritten letter, as many of these had seemingly fallen from the top of the stacks and covered the now-concealed maroon carpet adorning the sitting-room, all the while as the sounds of crinkled paper invaded the silence.

"Mrs Hudson, is that the *Daily Telegraph* I hear being crushed to death?"

Holmes' muffled voice echoed down the narrow hallway from inside his bedroom. Presently, a loud bang, followed by hurried footsteps, signalled the arrival of my friend as he dashed into the sitting-room.

"Watson! Was that not Mrs Hudson's delightful voice I heard just now?" he enquired with an intrigued expression on his face.

"She was here indeed," I replied smiling. "It would seem, however, that your recent lodging rituals are none to her liking." I stretched my arms outwards and looked at the littered surroundings with a half-mocking expression.

"Tut! Tut! Even *my* brain has a restricted capacity for collecting information. When that is occupied, I use other means of storage," he answered, looking around the room before laying his eyes on me with an impish smile.

"It's so good to see you Watson," he continued, "and I'm glad you took up my offer so eagerly." He walked forward and grabbed me by my shoulders, shaking me gently but in earnest. "How is the wife?"

To an unsuspecting visitor, it would have been impossible to tell whether my friend meant what he said. Even I, accustomed to Sherlock Holmes' distancing from the emotional qualities of man, was struck by his concern for my family affairs.

"Very well thank you. She is currently visiting her cousins in Wiltshire and will be back next week," I explained.

"Excellent! Then she will surely not object to my inviting you here for a day or two to occupy your time," he returned with the same mischievous grin on his face.

I have often remarked, in my previous accounts of our adventures, of my friend's capacity for altering his mood or attitude at the mere striking of a match. The strain between our bond, which I had begun to detect a while back, suddenly seemed to dissipate. Even his recent irritable behaviour appeared to vanish at our meeting, and although he would say nothing of his imprisonment in his room, I was wise enough not to ask any further.

"So you have a new case?" I asked, making my way to the sofa which had not been spared in my friend's quest for the acquisition of knowledge. Pushing away a pile of hastily bound letters and several crumpled newspapers aside, I settled down with a sigh.

"Careful, Watson!" exclaimed my friend, taking a sudden step forward. "You've just laid aside the scandalous letters of Lady Bamford to a senior politician. Not to mention the detailed article from this morning's gruesome discovery in Trafalgar Square." I picked up one of the newspapers to which he pointed and opened it where it had been folded. This is what I read in one of the main columns:

Trafalgar Square Murder
The body of an unidentified man was found early this morning lying at the foot of Nelson's Column. The victim, who appears to be just over fifty years of age,

was found wearing ragged clothes, with nothing more than a weathered and torn bag containing some scraps of food by his side. Scotland Yard officials are seeking information on the identity of the victim and have already established the circumstances of the man's death. Inspector Gregson is providing his invaluable professional experience by heading the case. He has confidently stated that the man is likely to be a criminal, and that the torn paper found clutched in his hand is indicative of a failed robbery attempt. An altercation of sorts must have ensued as the man assaulted an unsuspecting passerby, but ended up falling foul of his own criminal actions. Scotland Yard is confident that all the facts of the case will be brought to light following a thorough investigation.

"To battle, Watson! Trafalgar Square calls us!" cried Holmes. He dashed out of the room with such vigour that, without pausing to contemplate on what I had just read, I rose from the sofa and quickly followed my friend into the street outside.

The scene which greeted us when we arrived at Trafalgar Square was peculiar. A sinister silence seemed to have settled on this busy London intersection. Dark clouds hung low and a sense of expectation filled the air around us. Near the base of Nelson's Column, between two of the majestic north-facing bronze lions, we descried a large congregation of people that had gathered there. As we approached the crowd several police constables began pushing inquisitive members of the public away from the motionless body of a man that lay slumped on the ground with his back resting against the base of the monument.

The familiar small frame of Inspector Gregson, bending over the lifeless corpse whilst scribbling in his notebook, came into view. Presently, he noticed our arrival and greeted us with much enthusiasm and the unmistakable sense of relief in his smile.

"Mr Holmes! What brings you here?" he smirked, rising from beside the body and extending a hand towards us.

"Mere curiosity, nothing more," said my friend, shaking the inspector's hand with a distinct twinkle in his eyes.

"I will not deny it, Mr Holmes. I relish your participation in our cases," added Gregson.

"Excellent! Then you would not deny me a glimpse of the body?" asked Holmes, already making his way to the lifeless man. He bent down, extracted his lens and proceeded to conduct a thorough analysis of the entire corpse and its surroundings.

"Wouldn't you rather I let you know the facts before?" proposed the perplexed inspector, in the process of opening up his notebook to consult his scribbles. By now, Holmes was closely inspecting the dirty nails and fingers that gripped the torn piece of paper reported in the newspaper.

"I would much rather gather my own facts directly, Gregson." Holmes looked up at the inspector and smiled, before moving on to an examination of the man's head. By this time, the crowd had been pushed away from the area and the stillness in the air seemed to deepen. A few drops of rain started to fall, increasing the sense of gloom that lingered. An innocent victim, or a criminal dead by his own carelessness, was nevertheless a sad sight. The attire of the man was enough to indicate a solitary and poor life, one led on the rough London streets; a life of furtiveness and constant thieving, trying to survive the odds, only to end up at the mercy of a cruel twist of fate.

"Doctor, a moment if you please." Holmes had carried on with his analysis of the victim's face and momentarily looked at me with an intense stare. Leaving Gregson's side, as he started giving some generic orders to his constables, I walked towards my friend and bent down close to the body. I glanced at the man's particular characteristics. His face was lean with a rough stubble along the length of his square jaw. Deep creases surrounded his eyes, whilst his bony nose had been bruised. A strong smell of alcohol assaulted my senses, mingled with a distinct musty odour characteristic of a life lived under some rotting shelter in a forsaken alleyway. Holmes was pointing to a dark mark on the man's bald head. The few remaining wisps of dank, grey hair stuck firmly to the crimson wound on the pale skin.

"Any remarks?" my friend asked in a quiet tone.

I surveyed what looked like the result of a severe blow from some blunt weapon. A considerable gash ran across the scalp. Fragments of bone, most likely the result of a shattered skull, protruded through the lesion. Most of the blood had congealed, but a few drops were still fresh, giving a rough indication as to the time the injury was caused. Around the wound, the flesh was slightly swollen, whilst the crimson hue was slowly turning into a tinge of purple as a large bruise indicated internal bleeding.

"Time of death?" asked Holmes, as if he had guessed my thoughts, or most likely arrived at some conclusion himself.

"Given the appearance of the wound, I would say not later than ten o'clock last night," I replied, moving away from the corpse to survey the area around us. My eyes soon returned to the body, particularly to the paper clutched in the man's hand which, upon closer inspection, was actually two pieces stuck to each other. They appeared to have been torn off the top left corner of a document of sorts. There were some letters printed on the paper but, given the small size of the remaining pieces, it was difficult to make out what the contents might have been. As I glanced again at the gloomy atmosphere of Trafalgar Square, the crowd had dissipated and the silence seemed absolute. Gregson paced to and fro, consulting his notebook, whilst the other police constables made themselves look busy.

"What about the paper? Any ideas?" I looked back at the inspector in search of answers. He looked up, somewhat in a daze, and came forward shaking his head. He looked to where I pointed and snapped out of his inner thoughts.

"Ah yes! We believe it is nothing more than some pages from a book being carried by the passerby," remarked Inspector Gregson.

"What passerby?" asked Holmes, giving me a sidelong grin.

"Well," stammered Gregson, "The victim was clearly in need of money. Given his desperation, he must have assaulted some poor soul in the street and grabbed him, tearing away some pages of a book. So, they're not relevant to the case at hand. Though it is strange we haven't heard any report of an assault so far." Gregson's words trailed off as he pondered his own statement.

"Very strange indeed," proclaimed Holmes thoughtfully, as he rose and scratched his chin with a subtle hint of jest. His tone of voice was quiet, but filled with lighthearted mockery that went unnoticed by Gregson.

"Then with your permission, Inspector," said Holmes snapping out of his pretence, "allow me to keep these irrelevant pieces of paper for further consultation." Sherlock Holmes smiled at the Scotland Yard official, as he gently extracted the fragments from the dead man's tightly-gripped fingers. Having done so, he placed them with care inside his overcoat pocket.

"I hope to hear of any outcomes Inspector," said Holmes as he waved goodbye. I followed my friend across Trafalgar Square, and we soon disappeared into the bustle of a London morning along the Strand. We headed back to 221B, but my friend, in his usual manner of secrecy, said no more of the incident. Soon after, he left the lodgings once more leaving me alone with my thoughts. I neither heard nor saw any more of him that day and I confess that by the time evening came, I found myself exhausted with boredom and the lack of any adventurous engagements on the case at hand. It was almost midnight, and having heard no more of my friend, I retired to my old room to get some sleep.

When I woke up early the following morning, I was quite surprised to discover Mycroft Holmes in our sitting-room. I have remarked in some of my earlier encounters of that man's corpulent frame and overweight disposition. As I walked in the room, he had been sitting in my companion's favourite armchair next to the window, surveying the activities in the street outside.

"That man has a most intriguing gait disorder, wouldn't you say Dr Watson?" He kept his eyes on the street, but spoke as soon as he heard my footsteps entering the room. There seemed to be no sign of my companion anywhere in our lodgings, and unable to comprehend how the elder brother had found himself so unexpectedly in our sitting-room, I ventured to ask.

"Mr Holmes," I stammered, moving forward to where he sat, "what brings you here?"

"A trivial thing no doubt. I came to see my brother upon a matter of importance to the country, but it seems he did not return last night," he said as he gestured with his head towards the window, then turned round to look at me. There was a grin on his wrinkled face.

"I find you in good health sir." He laughed as I spoke and turned again to the view outside.

"Health is inconsequential Doctor. Man is a most fascinating subject to study at a distance." He gestured once more towards the window panes through which he had been looking. I bent down to follow his line of sight as the sun filtered through the dusty glass. On the farther side of the street, trudging in a northerly direction past our lodgings, was a man in a single dark blue overall, the colour of which was much faded and grimy.

"The victim of an unfortunate accident. Notice how he struggles with his left leg as he plods along the street, swaying from one side to another. Not to mention the recent addition of a nasty wound to his left shoulder."

"Why recent?" I asked, intrigued by his statement and analysis of the man's physical condition

"Notice how he swerves past other pedestrians, and carefully avoids contact on his left side. His right arm is placed slightly forwards in front of his chest, as if prepared to block a potential mishap, such as someone bumping into him and causing additional unwanted pain." Mycroft Holmes turned round and looked up at me with that same sharpness of expression which was so familiar and characteristic in the younger brother.

"Undoubtedly a retired sailor on his way to seek a new means of income," responded a gruff voice behind us. As I turned round, my eyes fell upon a scruffy-looking man with a long shaggy beard and a torn hat on a mass of grizzled hair. As he stood on the threshold of the room, I noticed he wore a tainted light brown coat, whilst his dark boots were caked with mud. His face, hardly distinguishable, was dirty and smeared with coal stains.

"The dark clothes and his unfortunate predisposition point to nothing more than a low-ranking veteran of the sea," he mumbled, as he took another step forward.

Beside me, Mycroft Holmes had remained seated, as he eyed the unpleasant intruder with a slight grin. I was alarmed by the invasion and suspected some sinister motive behind the man's sudden appearance in our lodgings. I stepped forward quickly, ready to push him back out into the street.

"Gently Watson!" uttered the man, raising his arms towards me in a gesture of surrender. "I am all too familiar with your skills as a soldier." He placed his right hand over his forehead and pulled at his hat. To my complete astonishment, that mass of tangled hair fell to the ground. He then proceeded to wipe his face with a grubby handkerchief and suddenly the veil of trickery faded away and the familiar face of Sherlock Holmes was revealed.

"Holmes! I thought you were some misguided tramp asking for trouble."

"Your reaction pleases me Watson," said my companion, as he walked inside and removed the rest of the disguise. He headed towards the mantlepiece and lit up his pipe. There was a subtle hint of disappointment and frustration as he noticed his brother sitting in his armchair, with no immediate intention of moving.

"Convincing as your disguise was, Sherlock, it is clear you have failed in your endeavour," grinned Mycroft.

Sherlock Holmes made no answer, and simply removed the pipe from his mouth and headed towards the sofa. He sighed and lay down lengthwise, resting his head on one of the arms still littered with scraps of paper. His older brother's grin did nothing but intensify. A childish disposition seemed to arise between the two, something unlike anything I had yet seen. The one ashamed of his failure, whilst the other triumphant over that misery. After a few moments of looking at his younger brother's behaviour, he attempted to console him.

"Come, come Sherlock. We both know you're not a man that gives up an unsuccessful chase so easily."

Mycroft Holmes rose with some difficulty from the chair and made his way laboriously across the room, through the maze of litter, pausing next to his dejected brother.

"Well, now that you are here, I can bring to conclusion my visit and allow myself to move onto other pressing matters."

The younger sibling shifted in the sofa, with his right arm covering his face, whilst Mycroft's voice boomed with the authoritative resonance that was so synonymous of the older Holmes.

"Sherlock, a matter has come to our attention from one of the highest offices in the government. A document of national importance went missing early this morning from the headquarters of the Quartermaster-General at the War Office."

My friend raised himself slightly from the sofa whilst his brother continued with what looked like the beginning of a new case and another line of inquiry for Sherlock Holmes.

"This document, of which the contents are not relevant to you, was drafted yesterday afternoon by Mr Jeremiah Tilbury, secretary to General Kenward. It was supposed to have been signed and delivered to the Office of the Prime Minister by Mr Tilbury himself, but until this morning no sign of Tilbury nor the document have been seen." Mycroft Holmes left the side of the sofa and walked towards the front door before turning round to eye his brother with an intense stare.

"Suffice to say Sherlock, the recovery of this document would be immensely appreciated by the government. In fact, I have personally arranged for a meeting with General Kenward at 11 o'clock today." Mycroft Holmes paused momentarily to consult his watch. "That leaves you just an hour to rid yourself of this shoddy appearance and go to Cumberland House in Pall Mall where, it is hoped, you shall gather all the necessary facts of the case. Good day to you."

As swiftly as he seemed to have appeared in our sitting-room, Mycroft Holmes vanished and left us two companions to ponder the scant details of this new line of inquiry. I looked at Holmes, whose shut eyes and frowning brows indicated some deep thought was being assessed. Whether he was pondering his brother's details of the missing document, or his apparent failure in bringing some resolve to the Trafalgar Square case, could not be guessed.

"Well Holmes? What shall we do now?"

"How many yards from the Trafalgar lions to Pall Mall, Watson?" remarked Holmes with a sharpness that echoed in the silence of the room. I admit he took me off guard, as he opened his eyes and stared at me, motionless but ready to pounce at my answer.

"I'm afraid I don't follow you, Holmes."

My friend rose and hurried across the room, toppling over a stack or two of newspapers onto the floor. He reached for the top shelf of the bookcase by the mantelpiece and extracted a folded map of London. He placed the worn contents on the only remaining available floor space and opened it up to reveal a faded illustration of the major roads, buildings and complex interweaving passages of the City Centre.

"Does it not seem too much of a coincidence," he began, as he knelt down over the map whilst running his hands over its surface, "that on the same day an important government document is missing, a body is found holding fragments of what look distinctly similar to official papers, a mere half a mile away?" He made a low rasping sound with his voice as he calculated on the map.

"Well Watson, I think we'll pay a visit to General Kenward after all and acquire the remaining details of the case. If you wouldn't mind calling a cab, I'll be ready in five minutes." He rose from the floor and dashed into his room, only to emerge a minute or two later completely rid of his previous attire. As he walked outside into Baker Street, he was the same Sherlock Holmes with his characteristic mischievous and gentlemanly demeanour.

Within a quarter of an hour we had made our way to Pall Mall, stopping in front of a towering façade of brown and white brick stone, with numerous windows overlooking the street. Having passed beyond the outer metal railings, we followed the path leading up towards a large black door, with two round bronze handles. Towards the left of the door, a plaque was attached to the wall, on which were engraved the names of all the departments within the War Office.

On any other day, even if my friend had decided to utilise his charms on the unsuspecting workers at this Office, it would nonetheless have been impossible to gain entrance to the building. The name of Mycroft Holmes, however, instantly brought us into the lavishly-furnished office of General Kenward himself. We sat in front of an elegant desk upon which writing implements and parchments were neatly placed in their proper sections.

Despite all its decorative furniture, towering bookcases, extravagantly framed paintings of past occupants and intricate chandeliers dangling from the ceiling, it was a lonely room. Its grandiosity failed to provide the warmth and comfort necessary for such a high-ranking position in the country. There was a smell of humidity mixed with staleness. Clearly, affairs involving politics and warfare had left their mark in more than just the sight of hefty volumes of government documents adorning two bookshelves at both ends of the room.

A few minutes passed, until we heard the distinct sound of several footsteps echoing along the vast, hollow corridor outside. The pacing was steady and relentless, making its way towards the closed office door, which suddenly opened to reveal two contrasting figures. The one, young and clearly occupying a clerical position of some sort, halted by the door and lowered his head. The other, who ventured inside and paused behind the desk, was tall, well-built, and with a somewhat irritable disposition complementing his elderly appearance.

However, all this went unnoticed at first, as both Holmes and I recoiled in surprise and disbelief at the sight of General Kenward. I confess that it was my initial belief we had just witnessed some abnormal occurrence in which the laws of nature had been momentarily suspended. There, in front of us, stern in his pride and pomposity stood the murder victim from Trafalgar Square. The features, which my friend and I had closely studied the day before, were all sculpted on that man's face. The bald head, square jaw and long droopy earlobes were all there before us on a living, breathing human being.

Glancing at Holmes, I could not fail to see that he was as equally surprised as I was, but a sudden glint in his eye soon made me suspect he had arrived at some resolution as to this impossibility before I myself could comprehend one. He broke into a smile and extended his hand in greeting. The other, haughtily, avoided my friend's gesture and sat down.

"Gentlemen, straight to business if you please." He spoke with a clarity that defied his advanced years. "As I'm sure you are aware, a document has been stolen from our office. Undoubtedly, that dratted Tilbury has snatched it for some financial profit or other. Suffice to say, my reputation hangs in the balance."

"Not the safety of the nation then?" interrupted Holmes with a hint of sarcasm in his voice. General Kenward was taken aback by the intrusion, evident from the astonished expression on his face.

"Well yes, yes of course," he stammered. "It is imperative that it is found and returned before any of its contents are exposed to some dangerous individuals or the public. This document is, after all, a beacon of hope that seeks to maintain peace with our neighbouring countries. It is a milestone in this Office's many years of service." He spoke with a sense of pride mingled with arrogance: a distinct trait undoubtedly accumulated through many years of occupying such a high-ranking position.

"Why do you so blatantly accuse your secretary of the crime? Do you have any evidence we may be privy to?" asked Holmes, maintaining his sarcastic tone. This behaviour from my companion did not go unnoticed by our client, who sighed deeply and demonstrated visible signs of frustration as his fidgety hands grabbed the edge of the desk.

"My secretary was the only person entrusted to take the document from my office straight to that of the Prime Minister's. As of this morning neither document nor Tilbury have shown up." His irritated voice rose gradually as he reached the end of the sentence. "Now, I believe you have come into possession of a scrap of the document. Is that not so?" he proclaimed shortly after, in a somewhat calmer tone.

"Yes indeed, but I fear I may have misplaced it," responded Holmes with an air of indifference. I stared at Holmes with incredulity at the remark, but was outmatched by the sheer disbelief, mixed with surmounting wrath, from the General.

"Tell me about your family General Kenward. Any siblings?" inquired Holmes, after a few moments of intense silence. Our client flew into a rage, he stood up and banged his hand on the desk.

"Ridiculous! Absolutely ridiculous! Your behaviour is most inappropriate sir. First you insult me with your banter then you deflect the urgency of this case on trivial matters."

"A brother perhaps?" persisted my friend. I knew at that moment what Holmes' game was. The precise similarity of physical characteristics between General Kenward and the victim found in Trafalgar Square was too much of a coincidence.

"What is that to you?" raged our client. Sherlock Holmes shifted in his chair, looking up at the ceiling in a nonchalant manner.

"General, I am accustomed to finding out all there is to know about my clients before embarking on a case. The information I ask for might be irrelevant to you, but it is crucial to me. Therefore, for the sake of this country's safety, I ask you again. Do you have any siblings?"

The General regained his composure and slowly sat back down. He straightened himself up, as was his custom whenever he began to speak.

"One brother, yes," he said, with some difficulty. "A hot-headed fool who never showed any willingness to preserve the dignity of the family or that of himself." He ended his bitter retort with a dismissive snort.

"You are therefore unaware of your brother's current whereabouts or state of being?" inquired Holmes, leaning forward in his chair and eyeing the man with intense scrutiny.

"Absolutely not! Petty family matters from impossibly foolish relatives have no place in my line of work. Our paths veered away from each other a very long time ago. What he does or happens to him is of no interest to me. Is that satisfactory?" The General's tone of voice was sufficient to indicate that any further line of questioning on such matters was most unwelcome.

"Quite," replied Holmes tersely.

The General cleared his throat and snatched some papers from his desk. The conversation had clearly damaged his dignity and thus he attempted to divert the exchange back to the matter of the missing document.

"Your brother, Mycroft, has assured me of your co-operation Mr Holmes, and that you will be able to assist me in finding the document," he managed to declare, after a few moments of oppressive silence. My friend leaned casually back in his chair, unimpressed. He said nothing but glanced this way and that as if pondering some internal struggle.

"Well Mr Holmes, can you help me?" This last remark was emphasised by a sudden look of uneasiness on the General's face. He leaned forward, looking at both of us in turn.

"My brother may have failed to mention the type of client I was to deal with but, for the sake of the country, I will endeavour to seek a resolution to your concern." Holmes smirked at the General before leaving abruptly.

No matter how ill-mannered our client may have demonstrated himself to be, it was difficult not to underestimate the influential powers he must surely have possessed over matters of the law. I was always in constant agitation at Holmes' behaviour in front of certain important figures, which might have resulted in serious consequences for him. This, however, did not seem to trouble him at all.

Before our departure from the War Office we paid a visit to Mr Tilbury's secretarial station. The windowless room was plain and devoid of any decorative grandeur found in his employer's office. An uninteresting wallpaper, bearing floral motifs, covered the walls as dark wooden beams ran across the ceiling, from which dangled an overworked gas lamp. A small cabinet, unpolished and much battered, adorned the rather gloomy atmosphere inside and, along with a dusty bookshelf next to it, was the only other piece of furniture in an otherwise lifeless room. A few candles sputtered weakly on the desk which had been pushed towards the side of the wall on our left.

As we entered, Holmes had instantly made for it, examining the piles of papers, documents and letters stacked on its surface. Smudges and small blotches of oil stained the entire length and breadth of the visible surface of the desk. With the use of his lens, he began an inspection of all the objects to be found there, but these he soon ignored for a particular blank patch facing the chair, which had been left unoccupied by the clutter around.

"Much can be glimpsed from the writing habits of an individual, especially if his occupation depends entirely upon it," he proclaimed, bending down so much that his nose almost touched the smooth surface.

"There is a considerable impression on this side of the desk, with a distinctly darker hue to the surface than the rest. You can see the outline of a large square-shaped object which, given the use of this office and its occupant, was most likely a typewriter." From one side of the desk, Holmes picked up several papers which had clearly not been handwritten. He sniffed at the papers and then bent over the desk to the oil stains and inhaled again. "Given the deep impression on the desk, its oily scent, which is also present on these papers, and the type of rough-edged lettering, I believe it to be a Remington Standard No. 2, 1878 model." Having concluding this rather superb deduction, he abandoned the desk for the bookshelf, turning his head one way and the other.

"The question now is, where is it?" he finally stated. With one last glance at the room, he headed back into the corridor with a swift step.

I followed Holmes out of the building as we rejoined the busy life along Pall Mall.

"You don't think the General is somehow ..." I began cautiously, trying to keep up with my friend's fast-paced stride.

"No, no I think not," interrupted Holmes. "His arrogance does not reach as far as criminal intent. Nevertheless, his indifference towards the wellbeing of his brother is most curious."

"Do you not think the General should know about his brother's death?"

"All in good time, Watson. A document is missing, remember? Time is pressing!" he grinned. We took no cab back to our lodgings, but rather walked straight towards Trafalgar Square, as it was Holmes' intention to survey the area one more time. Occasionally, as we passed a lamp post or a patch of uneven pavement, he would slow down and look at the ground before dashing onwards again towards our destination.

"Holmes," I ventured to ask after several minutes of brisk walking past other busy Londoners, "have you truly lost that piece of the document?"

Holmes chuckled.

"Me? Misplacing a clue? Unheard of Watson! I'm concerned at your lack of trust in me," he said jokingly. He chuckled once more: a rare trait in the stern, precise character of Sherlock Holmes. "Naturally not Doctor. I merely gave it back to the murderer."

The last statement bewildered me, but before I had time to inquire further what he meant, we arrived at Trafalgar Square. The sun was still concealed behind gloomy skies and the air was cold, but by the time we arrived at our destination we were both quite flushed, and the murky air had somewhat cleared.

The square was relatively quiet, with a few passersby going about their daily business. Had I not witnessed the dead body myself the day before, I would never have suspected that a murder had been committed. There was no trace of evidence that I could see which hinted at any gruesome crime, and what Holmes intended to glean from it was impossible to say. He immediately began an analysis of the spot where the man had been found. The only possible indication of some act of violence were two small stains on the ground, undoubtedly a result of the victim's head injury. These, Holmes was now examining with his lens.

"It is rather superficial to conclude that whoever stole the document committed the murder. We have our potential suspect, secretary Jeremiah Tilbury, and his involvement seems absolute," said Holmes, as he moved over towards the base of the column itself.

"Due to a lack of details, surely we cannot definitively conclude he was responsible for the murder," I challenged. My friend paused for a moment as if thinking to himself, then proceeded to a close examination of the stone tiles around the base where the body had been found.

"Well, given that Mr Tilbury was the only one entrusted with the document, he is the key to this mystery. We cannot hope to dispel it without first retracing the secretary's footsteps."

"How on earth can we do that?" I asked. My friend's suggestion seemed rather too ambitious and impossible, even for his skill. Holmes stood up and smiled.

"Observation, Watson. The most singular faculty of the human mind. Let us, for instance, start from here and begin our hypothesis," he said, pointing at the blood stains on the ground. "What can we infer by those marks and the position of the body?"

"That the victim must have confronted his killer and was dealt a severe blow to the head," I acknowledged.

"Let us therefore make Mr Tilbury our culprit," continued Holmes. "He steals the document from the War Office two evenings ago. He walks along Pall Mall, with the document under his arm, and into Trafalgar Square where, for some unspecified reason, he is confronted by General Kenward's wayward brother. An altercation of sorts ensues. Mr Tilbury, undoubtedly unaware of the existence of his employer's twin relative, believes he has been caught in the act and thus attempts a sudden, desperate move to run away, losing a fragment of the document in the process."

"The blow was severe enough to fracture the skull and cause internal bleeding," I stated, recalling the bruising around the man's head.

"That is remarkable, given the weight Mr Tilbury had been carrying." Holmes looked at me and must have realised the confused and questioning glance I directed towards him. "Our missing Remington Standard No. 2. The secretary took it with him the night he stole the document, no doubt to produce a fair copy in the relative safety of his lodgings. It was mere fate that brought the unfortunate brother into Mr Tilbury's exact path. The blow must have come from the typewriter he had been lugging all the way with him, swinging it sufficiently hard enough to kill an adult man. The marks are indisputable."

Holmes moved closer to the base of Nelson's Column and pointed at tiny dark specks on the stone. "Those oil droplets came from Mr Tilbury's writing machine the moment he brought it round onto the victim's head. I have managed to spot a trace or two along Pall Mall from his office to this spot. The scent is unmistakable."

"Remarkable!" I exclaimed, unable to contain my excitement at the numerous observations my friend was producing.

"A feeble attempt, but enough to clear some of the mystery ahead of us."

"How you managed to gather all these facts in a few minutes is beyond me, Holmes." My praise had clearly pleased the consulting detective mightily. He smiled and, as was customary upon such occasions, slipped both hands into his trouser pockets and inhaled.

"Mycroft might think my attempt in prowling the London streets last night was unsuccessful. Clearly he was wrong." He smiled once more and then proceeded with his explanations as he walked further away from the body's original location.

"Mr Tilbury might be a killer, but he is an inexperienced one. In his alarm, he failed to notice the torn piece and only realised so upon his arrival back at his lodgings. One cannot hope to successfully sell or exchange such a significant document with a piece of it missing. So having disguised myself as a beggar, a successful endeavour given your hostility towards me this morning at 221B, I headed back here last night and placed the fragments at the base of the Column. I waited far into the long, cold hours of night hidden in the shadows and watchful of every passerby, intent upon luring the culprit. For a time my intuition seemed to falter, until finally the bait was successful. A man with a long dark overcoat and a bowler hat almost down to his eyes came cautiously from the direction of Charing Cross Road. I watched his movements from behind the western fountain. Arriving at the base of the Column, he bent down and quickly scurried away."

"I played a hazardous game Watson, one that I'm not too fond of. I allowed potential evidence to be taken back by the perpetrator, but it was the quickest way to solving the mystery. Suffice to say, I followed the individual to a quaint little inn at the end of Duncannon Street on the corner of the Strand. He hurried along into the building and, until this morning, according to Wiggins and the others I placed on guard, had not yet emerged from his den."

With this conclusion he lit up a cigarette and leaned against the base of one of the majestic lions ever on guard at the heart of the City. I looked at my companion with renewed admiration, which I had not thought possible after the many adventures and exploits we had been through together.

"So what now?" I asked, after a moment of silence with only the constant bustle of London's streets filling the air.

"We shall bring the dead back to life!" he grinned, finishing his cigarette and walking away from the monument.

It took a lot of convincing and some harsh words were hurled in my friend's direction, but later that day Holmes and I found ourselves accompanied by General Kenward and Inspector Gregson at the entrance to Duncannon Street. One of the Inspector's officers patrolled the area whilst the rest of us stepped in front of a decrepit building which, although shabby in appearance, promised a welcoming stay to any stray traveller on a chilly evening. Light streamed out from the mucky windows and a roar of laughter and song burst out in unison from inside. The shabby sign above the door read: *Gibble's Retreat*.

"This is most improper behaviour Mr Holmes. A man of my stature in such a disreputable place," protested the General.

To this day I was convinced that, although he could have easily identified and apprehended the culprit, Holmes decided instead to play with the vanity of his client which he had found so loathsome. His face that day showed delight and satisfaction at the General's annoyance.

We all walked inside and found ourselves in a restricted parlour which, given its size and the already crowded gathering, turned the stifling air into a gradual feeling of suffocation. Our client seemed the most affected by this, but his predicament was ignored by Holmes.

The familiar characteristics of Wiggins, head of the Baker Street Irregulars, emerged from a throng of individuals, followed by two or three other boys of similar appearance.

"Upstairs, second room on the right Mr Holmes," he shouted, amid the drowning noise. He looked up earnestly at my companion, who in turn smiled and gave a few coins to each of those present, before they wriggled their way out of the inn.

"Gentleman, shall we?" asked Holmes with a grin, as he gestured towards a winding staircase at the back of the parlour.

We all followed and, as the sounds of the crowd slowly faded, we could only hear our own footsteps on the creaking wood accompanied by the occasion grumbling of the General. The corridor which greeted us was far less desirable than the parlour. Its desolate appearance and lack of light made it look more like an unearthly habitation than a place of rest in the heart of an urban city. Holmes paused in front of a shabby door and placed his right ear on its rough surface. We stood there in the gloomy silence for a long while until the General's temperament could not be contained. He pushed past the inspector and myself, stamping with his heavy boots on the rotten floorboards.

"I have had enough of these silly theatrical tricks, Mr Holmes. There will be repercussions!" Enraged as he was in his outburst, he had enough wits to keep his voice down so as not to be heard by any occupants in the room.

"Behind this door lies your disgraced employee and your prized item," whispered Holmes. My friend's statement had a most dramatic effect on our client as his eyes widened with astonishment.

"Tilbury!" howled General Kenward, as he pushed my friend aside and burst into the room with a roar. "Where are you? You accursed imp! Where have you hidden it?"

From inside the room emerged weak yelps as the General launched a reinvigorated outburst of rage.

"Lord save me!" squealed the voice of the secretary. "Torment me not dreadful apparition!"

"I'll torment you more than you can bear!" cried our client. By this time, the inspector and I had joined Holmes by the door and looked inside. Crawling to a corner of the room, in terror at the looming figure of General Kenward, was the frail form of Jeremiah Tilbury. Curly wisps of his dark hair stuck to the side of his sweating face. Small round-rimmed glasses perched on a crooked aquiline nose. His pale lips quavered uncontrollably as our client took a step forward threateningly.

He never got his chance of retaliation, for Holmes, having had his share of amusement, stopped our client from committing any foolish deed.

"Well Watson, General Kenward has certainly been of use on this case," whispered Holmes in my ear. "His spectral presence is most impressive."

The inspector intervened to secure his handcuffs on Tilbury's thin wrists. The typewriter, which Holmes had identified as the weapon used in the murder, lay on a small bed by the grimy window. A considerable dent had been made to one of its corners. Indeed, it was remarkable how such a frail individual could have wielded such a heavy object with the required force to silence another man forever.

Few words are left to me to recount what happened in the successive events. Following his arrest, Jeremiah Tilbury was given a life sentence in Newgate prison. The document, much to the satisfaction of the General, was successfully recovered from a safe compartment in the room at *Gibble's Retreat*, ready to be dispatched to some deplorable individuals with only the prospect of profit on their corrupt minds.

What his reaction was to his brother's unfortunate end I have no record of. However, it is a fact that his reputation remained untarnished after these events. He commended the collaboration of the police, and Inspector Gregson himself received much of the praise. To my annoyance, Holmes' primary involvement in the case went unnoticed, as no doubt our client intended to reciprocate the insolence sustained upon himself by some means or other. Thankfully, Mycroft Holmes' influence within the British Government assured me that his younger brother would suffer no retaliation for the manner in which he had dealt with the General.

That evening, I took leave of Holmes on his doorstep in Baker Street. As we bid each other farewell, he looked at me with his piercing eyes.

"Indispensable as always Doctor." He smiled and shook my hand firmly before heading back into the cluttered den of 221B. Little did I know what he meant and what bitter circumstances would lead us on to another case together.

The Stalker's Pride

It was during the final days of November 1888, that London was in the grip of an unusually bitter autumn. I had taken some days off from my medical duties to spend more time with Mary and visit her relatives, who lived far away from the dangers and hardships of this great city.

Having returned to London, one stormy afternoon I decided to pay a visit to Baker Street and find out how my friend had been passing the days. As I approached the familiar street, its welcoming aesthetic drenched in a torrent of incessant rain, a young boy bumped into me. His already ragged clothes were completely soaked and the matted hair obscuring part of his face would have made him unrecognisable had I not noticed the familiar features of Wiggins, leader of the Baker Street Irregulars who frequently offered their keen-eyed services during many of my friend's cases.

"Wiggins! What brings you to Baker Street on such a dismal day?" I asked loudly over the sound of the pelting rain on my umbrella. Seeing his shivering figure looking up at me, I moved closer to try and shield him from the downpour.

"Just the usual sir. Runnin' errands for Mr Holmes!" he replied, shouting at the top of his lungs. Although I have always known him for his energetic movement and jovial disposition, carrying out with vigour the many tasks entrusted upon him and his friends by my companion, that afternoon he seemed upset as if some fear was trailing him.

I asked him whether all was well with him, to which he looked at me with wide eyes and opened his mouth as if to speak. He hesitated, then, as if some thought had suddenly struck him, ran off into the drenched streets.

The horrible weather was soon locked outside as I was greeted by the familiar aspects of my old lodgings. It had been a few weeks since my last visit and a change seemed to have occurred to the warm and welcoming atmosphere that used to greet me whenever I walked up the stairs and into the sitting-room. I felt a mixture of nostalgia and discomfort, as if I was an uninvited guest in a place that, for many years, had been a home. The fireplace, which was rarely unlit, was as cold and unattractive as I had ever known. The room was dark, except for the feeble light coming in from the windows. The curtains had been pushed aside and a layer of dust had settled over the whole room covering the heap of papers and books littering both furniture and the floor.

I ventured further inside and the gloom only deepened. There was an eerie silence that seemed to haunt 221B. Outside of the windows the sun was nowhere visible behind the dark clouds overhead, whilst large drops of rain spattered against the dusty glass. As I surveyed the disorganised contents around me once more, a faint noise broke the silence of the room. From the kitchen emerged a weak light and I saw a bent figure at the table peering through a microscope. Stepping closer, Sherlock Holmes' familiar features came into view. His face was grim and his eyes stared intently down the lens. Although I had made my presence evident, he remained silent and deeply absorbed by his analysis.

In that light, I discerned a small piece of pale-coloured paper positioned under the microscope lens. His hands were both covered in thick woollen gloves, with additional fabric wrapped round each finger, making their use almost impossible. In his right hand Holmes clumsily held a small pair of tweezers with which he was attempting to make some slight adjustments to the triangular scrap before him. Beside him on the table lay open a small, leather-covered metal box, inside which lay a handwritten letter. Its top right corner had been carefully clipped off, as evidenced by the smooth cut. It appeared to be a letter written with exquisite calligraphic skills. Intrigued by the elegant script, I leaned forward and reached for the paper. Before my fingers touched the inside of the box, a hand clutched me sharply round the wrist. Holmes had abandoned the tweezers and held me at bay.

"It is not my purpose to attend an early funeral of the late Dr Watson," said Holmes in a cold voice. His eyes remained fixed to the microscope as I staggered back, somewhat flustered by my companion's words.

"Dimethylmercury. The letter has been dipped in that toxic solution. One touch to your skin and Death himself will follow you swiftly. I myself almost suffered serious damage by the fumes as I opened the box." As he said this, Holmes turned round to face me. He smiled weakly, and for the first time I noticed a redness around his moist eyes.

"The price for my lack of attentiveness," he proclaimed, as he raised his hand to point at the scarlet hues around his pupils. "The irritation makes my current investigation less than clinical, but whatever pain it brings, I must thrust it aside to gather as much data before the next blow falls."

He leaned back in his chair and sighed deeply, staring with vacant eyes at the paper fragment on display. I looked in earnest at him, and a sudden cold chill struck my heart. The gloominess of the lodgings, the deadly contents in the box, and my own companion's foreboding words all pointed towards one eventuality. The sinister force that had been following us for almost a year, ever since an old man had asked for the manufacture of a wooden diamond, had finally caught up with us.

All the other cases that had followed raced before my eyes, as my mind tried to fashion the links that connected them all together. Holmes seemed to notice my bewildered expression and smiled grimly.

"You understand then the possible meaning behind this box and the letter, Watson," he said.

"I think I do," I replied after a pause, struggling to speak, as my mind flooded with images of unseen figures lurking in the shadows and causing mischief wherever my friend and I made acquaintance with London's criminal world.

"I must say I'm rather disappointed that we cannot find the truth without assistance from anonymous letters," said Sherlock Holmes after a few moments of silence.

"But what does it say?" I asked, pointing at the contents of the box. Holmes removed his gloves, reached out for some papers scattered on the table and handed them over to me. Each page had rough scribbles on it, indicative of my friend's own handwriting.

"It just so happens that I have made myself a copy. I find it much more practical as a reference than having to handle one that would not get me past the second paragraph." He smiled once more and rose from his chair, pacing around the kitchen. Despite his calm tone, his physical behaviour spoke to the contrary. A nervous disposition seemed to have taken hold of him.

"Ever since I began my career as a consulting detective I have never failed to treat a single package I received without due suspicion. This was one of them." He paused and pointed at the box. For a moment, Holmes' countenance seemed to relax into a genuine smile.

"Even before I opened the box, the acrid smell emanating from inside was enough to raise the alarm and allow for the necessary caution to be applied."

"But why would someone send you a letter they never intended you to read? Why write it at all?" I glanced at the words on the papers, unable to fully read and understand what was being said.

"Ah, Watson. You do not perceive the subtle clues behind the commonplace. Clearly, the author meant to send some sort of message or warning. Whoever wrote the letter and laced it with acid, knew I would not fall into that trap, but in the event that I did, it would have meant absolute victory for them. On the other hand, my survival would mean the opening gambit in a chess game long in preparation. Perhaps the contents of the letter will enlighten you on this matter."

I glanced back at the letter my friend had transcribed. Leaning against the table, with much trepidation, I began reading the account before me.

Dear Mr Holmes,

I did not doubt that you would see through this toxic veil. Still, you cannot blame a man for his attempt. My compliments on your superb thinking and skilled deduction. I would dearly like to present myself to such an esteemed individual as yourself, but my work – as I am sure you understand – prevents me from doing just so.

I can however, indulge in some curious facts about what I am. Where to begin? I might call myself an admirer of your work, but then again that would not be entirely true. An avid follower of your methods perhaps? Certainly. Your chain of reasoning, the link by link process you boast about in your stories is truly fascinating. Your stories! Of course, I am naturally indebted to Dr Watson, without whom your exploits would have been concealed from me, except for the one or two cases in which I was somewhat involved. Let me direct you back to the case of the Bielski brothers. Such a sensational turn of events, but how could you possibly disregard the one riddle that brought you to the case in the first place? Who had notified Scotland Yard via telegram, about the overnight break-in at the abandoned house? Perhaps you may recall the old man visiting that wood carver's shop in Streatham Street?

Allow me to confess that I am no master of disguise, but even you failed to recognise my true identity when we finally shook hands and spoke to each other. Perhaps you might not remember, but I do. That day was the most joyous for me. After months of hard work, I had finally made an acquaintance of the great Sherlock Holmes. I now had but to tighten the noose around you and Dr Watson.

Every word I write, the more I hate this letter; but I hated even more the moment I saw you staring into my eyes. As thrilling as it was to speak to you, it was equally arduous and repelling. That indifference, that cold preciseness, devoid of human emotion. Pursuing case after case without a care of who lives or dies. Truly, you are indeed the calculating machine as remarked on by your companion.

It is with complete honesty that I claim to be no academic or mathematical scholar. Pardon me, but your exploits in previous cases were most entertaining. Suffice to say, I am sure the challenge against petty adversaries proved but a small distraction for such a great mind as that of Sherlock Holmes. I am no master criminal, nor intend to become one, but without first completing my vengeance, I see no future before me.

It was a desire of mine to expose you to the intoxicating fumes of Richard Stanbury's study. Naturally, I could not place myself in the line of investigation. An intermediary was necessary. Poor Mrs Stanbury. Such a beautiful creature, but such hatred for her husband. She came to see me once, and I might have suggested she place some naphthalene in the fireplace. She almost visited me a second time, but your untimely intrusion prevented her from doing so. Pity she had to succumb to the strains of prison. The food is most toxic I hear.

Had I been in a position to do so, I would have delayed or completely avoided delivering this letter to you. However, the circumstances have forced me to reach out and make myself known to you and the looming danger in which you and those around you find themselves. To atone for your wrongs there is nothing that you can do. You have but to await the impending judgement that was set in motion by your lack of dedication and interest in protecting the one client who genuinely sought your assistance.

Beware the shadow that lurks round the corner, the distant footstep behind you, the sudden warmth of blood gushing out of your body at the impact of a bullet or thrust of a knife during your nightly prowls around London. That joyous day is not far off.

Until then, may you ever live in fear of Death's presence.

The silence which followed was intense. Lowering the letter, I tried to comprehend much of what the author hinted at. Holmes looked at me intently, and after a short silence, he leaned forward.

"Well Watson, what do you make of it?"

"Where is Mrs Hudson now?" I enquired, suddenly feeling apprehensive for her safety.

"I have evacuated the landlady from the premises, as a measure of precaution," said Holmes abruptly.

"Has it come to that?" I asked, a sense of dread rising.

"I fear it has." Holmes paused and then looked at the box and the letter inside it. He pulled it towards him and turned it round as he closed the lid and looked back towards me.

"What do you make of the letter?" he asked once again.

"It all seems so odd. I do not really know what to say."

"Doctor Watson lost for words!" Holmes gave a nervous laugh.

"Strangely, I feel relieved that the mystery is finally starting to reveal itself to us." I sighed, as if this confession eased my heavy heart. "I admit that the strange occurrences on our recent cases have been constantly on my mind. The letter has finally proven what I had been fearing, that someone has been causing havoc around us. But what of this young man referred to in the letter, and the grudge its author seems to bear against you?"

"Our data is as yet incomplete and we are unable to determine specific reasons behind this," he replied solemnly. He took a deep breath and his voice instantly changed into a more confident tone. "Yet, now that the contents of the letter have revealed to us some of the motives behind the series of recent shadowy incidents, let us see what this box can reveal. For we are still far from discovering the mind behind these deadly tricks. It is possible however to begin fashioning the chain that will lead us to the very place from which the letter was written and eventually the individual himself."

"Impossible!" I exclaimed, incredulous at such a claim, even if professed by my esteemed companion.

Holmes smiled. He gestured at the unoccupied chair across the table, and once I was seated, he looked at the box and began conducting a series of deductions, the kind of which I had so often been privy to.

"That this was delivered in person and placed on our front door is unquestionable. Such deadly contents would not have been safe via the postal service. No, this was brought to us by the letter's author or some agent of his."

"Him?" I asked, with some surprise.

"Yes Watson. Whilst the opposite sex is perfectly capable of being the mastermind behind these recent incidents, the balance of probability is more in favour of a male criminal. Besides," and he turned the box round to face me and re-opened the lid to reveal the toxic letter inside, "look at the particular pressure applied to the *p*'s and *d*'s in the words. Not to mention the angular strokes persistent throughout the whole letter, indicative of a man's handwriting."

I bent cautiously forward, following Holmes' precise explanations as to the specific calligraphy employed. Having been given a satisfactory answer, I leaned back in my chair.

"Wiggins himself has testified to seeing a man placing the box on our doorstep."

"Wiggins? I saw him just now. He seemed awfully put out by something," I said, as I recalled my meeting with the boy.

"Ah yes. That might have been caused by the sight of the figure of an old man who came creeping up to the main door and seemed to be up to no good." At the mention of an old man, Holmes smiled impishly at my astonished expression. He closed the box once again and proceeded with his analysis.

"The outside environment, including the weather and the atmosphere itself, can leave its mark on an individual and an object alike. The base of the box has been soiled with small fragments of leaf and mud. In such an industrialised city as London, it is hard not to imagine this package coming from a park or a garden. Let us suppose the latter as the start of our working hypothesis. Our stranger, for whatever reason, placed the box upon the ground in one of the many gardens around London. He then took the box and made his way to Baker Street to deliver the parcel. But which route did he take?"

My friend paused and pushed the box closer towards me, leaning forward and pointing at a specific section before continuing with the examination.

"Notice the dampness from tiny water particles on one side of the box. It has been raining has it not? Clearly, whoever brought this carried it underneath the arm, protecting most of it from the downpour. Yet, notice how the top part of the box is less wet than the side. Today is also rather gusty, a strong wind blows from the west. Thus our stranger must have taken a left turn at some point during his journey and faced the oncoming wind which drove the rain against this side of the box which soaked up more than the top part. So we can safely assume that our man has come somewhere from the east side of Baker Street. Our search is slowly narrowing itself down."

"Extraordinary," I muttered in awe at my friend's precise and calculated thoughts. Holmes smiled at the compliment.

"Watson, we can further reinforce this idea by the presence of distinct dust particles along this edge, which have attached themselves to the heaviest water droplets. I have had some time to analyse these specks which are a very particular type of limestone. The North London Hospital lies on the corner between Euston Road and Gower Street. There just happens to be some restoration work going on to the hospital's memorial stone just outside the main building overlooking Euston Road.

The fragments are unmistakable, and the peculiar colour is synonymous with that of Portland stone, which has been utilised for St. Paul's, the Tower and many other majestic buildings that currently adorn this great city."

Holmes paused to regain his breath, eager as he was to press on in outlining his reasoning and analysis.

"Let us therefore assume that our stranger has taken a sharp left from Gower Street into Euston Road, where the westerly wind has helpfully aided us in our pursuit of whence this box came. It is not too difficult then to follow the natural route to these lodgings if one were to find himself at Euston. The Marylebone Road provides the swiftest and most direct course towards Baker Street. We must therefore concentrate our search within Gower Street where, by our careful and calculated thought process, one may find Bedford Square Gardens. This is the most likely spot in which the box was laid down, thereby accumulating the soil and leaf that has enabled us to start fashioning our link of investigation."

It was still utterly remarkable how my friend always managed to surprise me with his precise deductions. What usually seemed like an impossible task was soon rendered an obvious fact by the brilliant mind of Sherlock Holmes.

Presently, as I lay pondering on these new details, he once again pulled on the gloves and carefully extracted the letter from the box.

"Now," he said quietly, as he held the letter up to the faint light coming from the small kitchen window. "We have the name of the street, but we still require a more precise identification of the location from which this originated."

With some difficulty Holmes produced his magnifying lens. "There are some faint indications where the ink on one side of the paper has dried up more quickly than the other." He handed over the lens and invited me to examine the writing.

"Look at the way in which the ink has had time to really soak into the thick gauge of the paper, whilst on the left there is much less ink that has sunk into the surface. Also, the ink on this side is considerably lighter than the other, which points towards the distinct possibility that the author faced north, with a window accessible to sunlight on his left which allowed the ink to dry much quicker on one side. Thus our mysterious correspondent may reside somewhere on the east side of Gower Street. Also," and this time he sniffed rapidly, at both letter and box, "they smell musty, which means it was probably stored in a small, humid place. Shall we?"

Holmes removed the gloves and rose from the table. He pointed towards the door which led to the stairs. I immediately followed him out of the kitchen, feeling a rush of energy surging through my body. Holmes raised his arm, bringing me to a halt on the landing.

"We are about to embark on the most dangerous of expeditions, Watson," he said in a whisper. "I must ask of you to follow my every lead without protest and strictly to the letter, for your own sake and mine. Are you still eager to pursue this matter with me?"

"Absolutely," I remarked, even though his somewhat foreboding words had increased both the thrill as well as the fear that seemed to be following us. Holmes smiled, despite his anxious expression. He hurried back inside, picked up his coat and placed his revolver in one of its pockets.

"I would rather we walked to our destination than board a cab, Watson. I should like to inspect the route for any further data we might require," Holmes announced, as we emerged from the warm lodgings and out into the miserable weather.

It was a long and dreary journey as we hurried along the interminable Marylebone Road, until we arrived at the intersection between Euston Road and Gower Street. The incessant rain and wind had hindered my friend's investigation, and no doubt washed away any potential clues that might have been left on the road. Once or twice upon our way I happened to notice, or thought I noticed, a hansom following our route. Every time we halted, there it stood a short distance behind us. On we went and so did it. It never overtook us, but every now and then took to turning into one of the adjoining streets along the Marylebone way, only to re-emerge once more right behind us.

We passed the limestone monument in front of the North London Hospital. Despite the rain, remnants of the dust from the uncovered restoration works were still falling and being blown across the road, as Holmes had correctly guessed. As soon as we made our way round the corner into Gower Street, the wind dropped, but the rain persisted. Here, Holmes walked cautiously along, analysing each of the buildings on our right for any potential indication as to the whereabouts of the letter's origination.

By the time we had reached half the length of the street, the afternoon was turning into evening. The light was failing and the rain had become a gentle drizzle. The urban roar of London's inhabitants had long started to abate as we found ourselves at the lower end of Gower Street where an ominous silence had settled. Shortly before five o'clock, Holmes halted underneath a gas lamp post. He pointed slightly ahead and to the right at a massive structure covering a large expanse of land. Its towering walls and high windows housed the peak of human knowledge and discovery.

"The British Museum," whispered Holmes.

"Is it significant?" I inquired, following from my companion's low tone of voice.

"To humanity? – Quite indispensable. To our current investigation? – Perhaps."

He walked forward and crossed the street. At that instant, the quiet was broken by the distinct sound of horses coming to a halt behind us. With the oncoming darkness, a fog had settled around us, thick enough to prohibit me from seeing more than a few yards in any direction. Holmes was by now lost in a hazy veil.

Across the street I found him resting against the last building adjacent to Bedford Square Gardens. His movements were furtive and he avoided raising his voice above a whisper. He pointed back at the other side of the street from where we had come. Just a few yards ahead, before another road turned east towards the British Museum, a warm light emerged from a small window, penetrating the fog outside. A building on the corner, with a wooden façade, contrasted sharply with the rest of the street's dark-hued houses. Beside the window, a small door with a faded sign was all that the available light permitted us to see. It was clear however, from Holmes' strained neck and intense gaze that we had reached the supposed location from which the letter had been written. As my eyes adjusted to the darkness, I could discern a familiar insignia on the door: two little angels facing each other, one pointing and the other kneeling in submission, surrounded by the same ivy-like floral design. That same mark, which had haunted several of our recent cases, was once again the cause of our current line of investigation.

"Watson, you remember the condition on which I brought you here?" whispered Holmes. I nodded decisively and followed him once again across the street and into the Gardens. We sought concealment under an elm tree beside the main gate. Quiet and peaceful as the Gardens were, it was a dismal place to be in at that moment. Water drops fell constantly on our heads from the leaves above us, and the chill began to bite into our bones.

"Meet me in ten minutes, at the bakery on the corner with Tottenham Court Road," said Holmes suddenly, and dashed back into Gower Street towards the building. Calling after him in a hoarse voice proved to be useless. He ignored me and soon vanished into the thick wall of fog.

The fear, which steadily grew as we made our way there, only increased with the ever-present threat. The anonymity of the letter's author, some calculating force ready to thwart our plans of bringing any culprits to justice, and the inability to comprehend what and when the next criminal blow would fall, was a growing peril to the safety of us both, and especially to Sherlock Holmes, whom the letter had so viciously attacked and promised swift and deadly retribution.

A few minutes had passed when a door burst open and a scuffle broke out in the darkness. Shouts echoed through the street before me and the noise of a horse-drawn cab echoed down through the fog. Shadowy figures flitted across the light from the building. Instinct and experience of war compelled me forward to investigate, but remembering my companion's strict instructions I retreated across Bedford Square and soon found myself in the intersection with Tottenham Court Road, where Londoners still occupied themselves with their end of day business.

Pausing in front of the designated bakery, whose occupants were in the process of closing its doors and windows, I looked round for signs of my friend. Breathing heavily in a state of agitation, I ran up and down a few yards in the hope of seeing Sherlock Holmes alive and safe.

It was well past the allotted time when a voice called out behind me.

"Watson," it cried out faintly, as Holmes' bent figure staggered forward from the gloom. His right hand was placed over his lowered head. He faltered and almost fell to the ground were it not for my sudden lunge forward to support him.

"Baker Street, Watson," he urged weakly. Calling a cab, we made our way back to 221B where, before desperately asking what had occurred, I was able to inspect and medicate the wound Holmes had sustained. An ugly gash along the parietal bone of the skull was evident. It was not deep but required disinfection and careful treatment. Holmes was silent during the whole procedure and, once done, he staggered clumsily forward and slumped onto the armchair in the sitting-room.

I knew that any questions I asked at that moment were of no avail. He would, in all likelihood, spend the night thinking over the events of that afternoon; weighing the situation and attempting to arrive one step closer to the truth.

He reached for a small box on the mantelpiece beside him, extracting a small syringe from inside; and for the first time in all my years with Sherlock Holmes, I uttered no word on the matter.

The Blind Prisoner

It was a time of hardship. It was a time of trial. Ever since Sherlock Holmes had received the lethal package on the doorstep of 221B, our paths had been leading towards predictable misfortune and deadly perils. It is thus with a heavy heart and a scarred memory that I begin this account in which my companion and I headed towards the very roots of the mystery that stalked our every step.

I woke up in darkness, or so I thought. My senses were numb. Hearing was the only remaining physical faculty I possessed, but even that seemed to be failing. An irritating sound of dripping water echoed in my ears. Slowly, as my mind came back to life and regained some measure of consciousness, I felt the hard cold ground beneath me and the drenched wall I was leaning against. The air turned stale and humid, as the ominous droplets seemed to intensify. An impenetrable blackness still lingered in front of my eyes, but my ears began to clear and my sense of touch grew stronger. Given the moist air and the splashes which echoed abruptly on stone, I surmised I had been thrown into a confined space, a small underground chamber.

    A dull pain throbbed steadily in my lower back, round to the left side of the abdomen. My weak attempts to struggle to my feet were inhibited by the sudden spasm of aching tender muscles. Breathing heavily, I lay still and rested once more against the wall with arms lying weakly over my lifeless legs. As I tried to recall the events that had flung me into that ghastly place, a dimness settled before my eyes. My head sagged over my chest whilst a murky blend of shadows slowly pierced the blackness, until the dark scarlet hue of two blooded and blistered hands took shape in my mind. The congealed blood, stuck around my fingernails and over the knuckles, reflected off a bright source of light which, upon raising my head, seemed to be coming from a narrow window high up behind me. As the darkness was lifted, so did the hazy chamber around me become clearer. It was indeed as gloomy and repulsive as I had imagined; the rough stones covering the floor, the rusty pieces of metal hanging from the mouldy walls and the cramped conditions. Nonetheless, the light failed to penetrate the darkness that still lay heavily on the other half of the chamber, and where I assumed a door stood. A small, rotting mattress on a crumbling metal frame lay on one side of the chamber, half-covered in shadow. Its dirty decrepit appearance failed to invite even the most desperate of individuals to seek any rest upon it.

At that moment, the fair smile of my wife appeared in my thoughts. Her tender glance and gentle disposition brought me comfort in that den of despair. However, the light on her expression soon turned dim. Her face became pale with angst and her eyes transformed into a doorway of fear. "Mary!" How she must have felt at my sudden and unexplained disappearance, I could not guess.

Forcing away these visions, my will hardened. The desperate need to escape and find the safety of my home took hold of me. I peered forward, attempting to pierce the shadowy veil, but a sharp onset of pain soon forced me backwards. Groaning loudly, heedless of the quivering silence, the monotonous dripping of water was disturbed by a low scraping sound along the floor, somewhere behind that wall of blackness before me. Gripped by a sudden sense of danger, I pushed myself further against the cold wall whilst attempting to deaden the pain.

Several soft rustles broke out. Something was lurking within the chamber. My hearing had improved considerably by now and I could clearly distinguish the slow agonising breaths of a human being. As I lay there, motionless, listening to every sound, several incoherent moans broke out. They were broad and deep, suggestive of a man trying to communicate. The moans persisted, until I began to comprehend what he was saying.

"G-Gower … house," exclaimed the weak voice.

Instantaneously, my mind fled back to the strong smell of gunpowder, the blinding flash and the rush of fire and smoke that had suddenly engulfed the room I was in. A copy of *The Strand*, which I had found moments prior was torn from my grasp. The stacks of printed papers and wooden desks flew and scattered around me. The force of the scorching blast threw me back against the door, before I collapsed back onto the splintered floor. My senses began to fail, as the turbulent noises raged on, until powerful hands pulled me away from the turmoil and into the cold night. My mind wavered on the edge of consciousness as I found myself on a dark, fog-enshrouded street corner.

Plumes of black smoke were streaming out of the burning building from which I had just been dragged. The street sign above me, now almost entirely blackened, read: 'Gower

Street'. At that moment, I felt myself being pulled to my feet by two individuals and pushed roughly into a nearby carriage. Momentarily fighting off an overwhelming faintness, I peered painfully back towards the street and saw Holmes' motionless body being lifted up and carried, before being flung beside me.

Holmes! My mind raced back to the present as I recognised the familiar voice of my companion moaning in that solitary chamber.

"Watson," he said in a weak tone, as he moved painfully and crawled slowly into the faint light. His clothing was torn and singed. Substantial bruising covered his bare forearms, but the most distressing features were his eyes. They were closed shut with a coating of grime, while reddened blisters covered his face. Sherlock Holmes, whose faculty of observation was unparalleled, was missing his most singular sense – sight.

Undoubtedly, our second visit to the premises in Gower Street, which had turned out to be a printing house, had ended in disaster.

Holmes slowly rose to his feet but wandered aimlessly, weaving this way and that in order to follow the sound of my voice. Despite my own acute pain, I lurched forward in much the same way, taking his arm and gently guiding him back to rest against the wall next to me.

"It's good to know you still live Watson," he said amid his heavy breathing. I looked at my companion with pity and dread; the stalwart figure of the great consulting detective reduced to such a helpless state. "Fear not my friend, I'm not as witless as I look," he gasped and then smiled as if sensing my concern.

"What happened last night and what is this abysmal place?"

"Two most pressing questions Doctor, of which the second may quite readily be resolved. Would you like to know my thoughts and judge whether Baker Street's prying detective has not completely lost his intellect?" He smiled, less painfully this time, yet his eyes remained closed with his head resting against the wall. His breathing had now returned to normal.

"I should like nothing more than some light on this mystery Holmes," I admitted. My friend coughed and, having assumed a similar resting position as mine, with his arms splayed carelessly to the sides of his outstretched legs, he began his account.

"After our incendiary visit to that private printing house in Gower Street, the carriage which brought us here took quite a direct route. There were a total of three changes in direction during a journey that lasted a good twenty minutes or so. There are two cracked granite blocks at the Bedford Square Gardens intersection. These the carriage drove over as we started off on our journey, providing a clear indication as to the direction the driver had taken. Thus, given our departure, we took a southerly direction along Bloomsbury Street, before veering towards the eastern end of Oxford Street."

Holmes stopped abruptly. A coughing fit had seized him and it was some time before he was able to continue talking. His throat, irritated by the violent coughs, made his voice even more feeble than before.

"At that Oxford Street crossing there is *Gribble's*, a little coffeehouse serving a quite distinct type of coffee blend. Its strong, dark roast odour is unmistakable at any time of day. After a short while there was some hesitation in the direction. The horses slowed down, but our course kept a fairly straight route towards High Holborn. That is a long stretch of road and we took no sudden turnings either way."

Although Holmes' voice was hoarse, he still spoke with that same lucidity and preciseness that was typical of his usual process of deduction.

"My calculations as to whether we were in the right place were soon to be confirmed, but I had already begun assessing other potential routes had we indeed taken a different turn instead of High Holborn. You must know Watson, that to the south side of Holborn lies the last-standing Inn of Chancery, an illustrious building constructed during the Tudor era. There, a gentle old soul bellows all day trying to sell fresh fish from the river, and his raspy voice reaches the highest of notes and pierces even the busiest of streets. One could therefore not fail to hear his cries above the galloping hooves and grating carriage wheels as we passed him by. Thus I was able to confirm my original hypothesis. After almost a quarter of an hour we came to a halt and both of us were dragged outside into the dark night before being thrust into this building. Given our current predicament and general indication as to our route, I welcome you to Newgate prison. Charming." He ended his deduction with a sigh. I smiled at his last remark. It was heartening to see Holmes maintaining his sarcastic humour during such a dire situation.

We lay there under the beam of light, with the occasional drop of water invading the silence. I was still attempting to piece the fragmented thoughts from the other night, when there appeared a glow in the darkness before us. Somewhere outside the chamber, a lantern had been lit and the light grew ever stronger as it approached. The grated door itself became visible: a series of rusted pieces of metal intersecting each other to form a decrepit gate.

Beyond it there appeared a corridor which seemed to be as dank and squalid as that present abode we found ourselves in. A clattering noise was followed by the squealing hinges of some other gate being opened and clanged shut, then echoing loudly through a vast, hollow hall. The deep rumbling sound was ominous. The warm glow of the light increased, reflecting off the dripping walls and rusting iron bars. Holmes struggled closer to me, leaning slightly sideways.

"Observe Watson," he whispered in my ear. Just at that moment, the approaching figure bearing the lantern came into view. Although the light furnished some further details of the chamber, the shadowy form before us had carefully placed it away from any face which lay hidden in the darkness. I gazed at the doorway and discerned the faint outline of an upright shape wearing a long coat which swayed behind as it moved. Two hands protruded from the sleeves, one holding the lantern and the other reaching for the door.

I held my breath. Next to me, Holmes stiffened. Unable to see what I was witnessing, he undoubtedly opted for his sense of hearing to glean any revealing information about our visitor, who in turn paused and began to whisper a sequence of phrases, inaudibly at first, in a guttural tone of voice. Eventually, a comprehensible structure began to fashion itself.

There was a persistent rhythm to those words, shaping themselves into an incantation of sorts.

> The time has come,
> the deed is done.
> Revenge at last,
> for wrongful past.
> From Horsham came
> Poor John the tame,
> betrayed by friend
> to cruel end.
> You thus shall fade,
> by doom now laid
> beyond this gate
> where gallows wait.

Having uttered those foreboding and cryptic words, the shadow stooped for a moment before bringing the lantern back up towards the upper part of the door. It stood there, clutching the rusted iron bars with its other hand. Its face was still veiled in shadow, but I could sense how the visitor looked in our direction with a malevolent stare. A few suppressed breaths escaped from the shadow which left no doubt in my mind that whatever was haunting our chamber was undoubtedly human. It lingered there for a moment, before turning round and, with the lantern cleverly handled, vanished from my sight.

Again silence reigned. The dripping had momentarily ceased and the gloom felt even more oppressive. Trying to recollect the scant details of our visitor's appearance and actions, I turned towards my friend to describe what I had seen.

"Holmes …" I began.

"The tapping Watson, the taps!" exclaimed my friend with agitation, as he shook my arm mercilessly. I thought he had fallen into a state of lucid delusion, but before I could ask him what he meant, he lunged forward, crawling along the rough floor towards the darkness. After a while, the grunting and puffing suddenly stopped. Holmes had clearly reached the gate.

Shortly after, the same noises disturbed the silence as he made his way back beside me. He breathed heavily and his whole frame trembled, for the exertion had been too much a strain on his crippled body.

"Holmes," I began again, "there was someone here, cloaked and gaunt …"

Again, I was interrupted by Holmes as he extended his left hand towards me. It was tightly closed and made its way down my right arm, before the contents dropped into the palm of my hand. I recoiled at the cold touch of the pieces which landed on my skin. I picked up one piece with the thumb and forefinger of my left hand, feeling the rough-hewn roundness of it. As I brought my hand close before my eyes I found what looked like small delicate stones.

"Seeds?" I uttered in my bewilderment.

"Orange pips, Watson. Five of them." Holmes' voice had regained some of that clarity that was characteristic of his nature. I looked at him with a questioning glance, until it suddenly struck me.

" 'From Horsham came … Poor John'," I whispered, recalling the stranger's ominous declaration. "Holmes, that copy of *The Strand* …," I continued.

"Yes, Watson. It seems that your popular stories recounting our exploits together have been enjoyed by our enemies too."

A chill ran down my spine as I recalled the tragic circumstances that had brought me to write about that case in *The Adventure of the Five Orange Pips*. A prospective client had walked into our lodgings, seeking the help of my friend.

John Openshaw was as innocent as any other young human being, but his uncle's exploits in Horsham had brought about inevitable vengeance by dangerous individuals.

"I failed that boy, Watson," proclaimed Holmes. My thoughts were broken by his statement. "His death has been on my conscience ever since," he continued.

On that stormy night just over two years ago, in the comfort of 221B, Holmes had assured our client of a successful resolution to his problem. The young man had gladly agreed to follow my friend's instructions in avoiding any untimely misfortune. Yet, as fate would have it, or rather the cruel mind of the criminal, John Openshaw's body was found the next day under Waterloo Bridge. The newspapers had reported the discovery as a tragic accident, but Holmes and I knew the terrible truth behind it – it had been murder, but the culprits were never caught. However, by some fated twist of chance, the vessel in which they had attempted their escape, had foundered in rough seas and their death was assured.

"Someone has been playing a long game with us, Watson, ever since we heard of that old man in the woodcarving shop and his words to Thomas Eldridge: 'The time has come'. That toxic letter I received, the resentful tone, the deadly threats, the accusations. Clearly someone blames us for the death of young John Openshaw. Me more than you, undoubtedly."

I let his words sink in. No matter how hard it was to believe, I could not help feel we had finally exposed the mystery that had been haunting us throughout these last few cases. The only riddle that remained now was to discover who was the cause of our troubles.

"Do you think that this stranger here today was one of his ruffians?" I asked after some moments of silence.

"No, no, I think not. I think our enemy has come himself, and alone, to gloat over our defeat and his triumph. He thinks his victory is assured and that our only way out of here is through the tightening of a noose round our necks." Holmes cried in pain as he repositioned himself to rest against the wall.

"But how did we end up here, and how are we going to get out?" I implored, feeling an overwhelming sense of fear gradually rising at the thought of an inescapable death.

"Holmes, the gallows lie before us!"

"Gently Watson," he said quietly, holding his head in both hands. He winced in agony, but the spasm soon passed. "All in good time Doctor."

The light around us seemed to dim once more as my mind drifted off into convoluted fits of restless slumber. Waking up brought no relief from the terror that had taken hold of me.

Holmes seemed to be asleep, resting his head against the wall. The silence seemed to invade the corridor and halls beyond our chamber. No sound or any other light filtered through. I could not say for how many hours we remained there, half-alive, waiting for a dreadful blow.

As I was about to fall into another restless dream, I woke up, suddenly alert. My heart beat rapidly as I sat motionless and tense, expecting some sudden doom. A loud noise from far away had disturbed my mind. I was ashamed of the terror that I felt, not only for myself but for the wellbeing of my friend too.

"Holmes, this seems to be leading towards unforeseen dangers and I dearly wish to see the end of it. But in your condition ..."

"Hush Watson! We find ourselves upon the threshold of a great revelation which might bring us to the unveiling of this mystery that has stalked us for these past months. Or else, we will fail so terribly that Death will find us all the more swiftly."

He spoke gravely, but truthfully. I was as eager to banish this persecution as much as Sherlock Holmes, but his words were nonetheless full of foreboding.

"Here are the facts as best as I can understand them." He took a few deep breaths before he continued. "It is no secret that there has been some sinister force thrusting these cases and circumstances upon us. Now we know that this unstoppable creature of imagination is merely a man; an individual that believes he has been wronged due to our inability in preventing poor John Openshaw's murder. He has outsmarted us, for now. Following his failed attempt in poisoning me through the letter, he has finally succeeded in cornering us and assuring both our deaths through the rope. I say for now because he has not yet secured such a definitive victory that he is above failure. Our precarious trip to his private printing house in Gower Street was not without its rewards. Our stalker has powerful friends who are able to lock us up without the proper procedures. I wonder where Gregson or Lestrade are?"

Holmes paused momentarily, and mumbled something to himself. He seemed to be reflecting on what he had just said.

"Remember the letter which spoke of my encounter with this stalker? I have been thinking about that precise point for many days now and I believe I may have an indication as to his identity."

This was undoubtedly a significant revelation, but at that moment I felt there were other more urgent matters.

"Now what Holmes? Death seems within reach. I am suffocating in this miserable place." My voice quavered in desperation.

"Take heart Watson, for unwise are those who despair at the sight of an obscure path before them," replied Holmes.

His words were of little comfort in that oppressive gloom.

"We have little time on our hands Watson. At any moment we might be dragged out and taken to the gallows. Are you able to move?"

"I must, even though the pain is unbearable. The thought of leaving this place is enough to urge me forward," I declared.

"Excellent Watson! Always the brave soldier." Holmes raised himself, pulling me gently up with him. "Are there any rags we can use?"

"There's a mattress with a tattered sheet," I replied, glancing at the mangled bed.

"Then I must ask you to suppress your agony and conceal the gate with that."

I left the wall and headed towards the bed. Having pulled the sheet away, I broke off a few pieces of metal from the rotting frame and made for the other side of the chamber.

Moving towards the gate was agonising, but the hope of escaping the gallows gave me enough strength to perform the necessary task. I did what was asked of me and spread the sheet along the low gate, affixing it with the metal fragments to cover up the view of the chamber from outside.

"Now we must place the bed in front of the gate and lie in wait." Holmes' hoarse voice echoed in the darkness. Despite its flimsy appearance, it was a long time before we managed to position it just a short distance away from the entrance.

Regardless of his impediment, Holmes assisted me in dragging the metal frame lengthwise across the chamber in front of the gate. By the time we were done, I lay shuddering in the dark, out of breath and in severe agony.

"My apologies Watson for all this hardship. One last act before hopefully getting out of here." As I rested against the side of the gate, I saw Holmes crawling slowly forward, reaching out his left hand in an attempt to locate me. As pity mixed itself with sudden resolve, I strained myself forward and caught his arm. We made our way to the centre of the chamber with the bed between us and the gate, and waited.

How many hours had passed since we lay there, concealed by the impenetrable darkness, I could not guess. I had been looking back towards the gentle stream of light that fell from the high window onto the back of the chamber, when the dull clang of a gate down the left-hand side of the corridor disturbed the silence. The dull stamping of footsteps approached and an orange glow became visible behind the sheet. Then, a silhouette, appearing to hold a small lantern and wearing the cap of a prison guard came cautiously forward. It stopped.

"Oi! What are you two up to in there?" cried the rasping voice of the guard. He cursed and fumbled with his keys before he found what he was looking for and unlocked the gate. He pulled aside the sheet as he raised the lantern in front of him, and took a step forward.

"Now!" shouted Holmes, as we both gripped the side of the bed and pushed it as hard as we could, driving it against the legs of the guard. With a loud shout, he lost his balance and was thrown over, hitting his head on the hard cold ground and lay motionless and unconscious.

The guard's bunch of keys clattered harshly against the ground followed by the loud crash of the lantern as it slipped from his grasp. The sound echoed through the hollow chamber and out into the corridor. I stood silent and tense, listening only to the rapid beating of my heart. The noise brought with it no further cries or running footsteps from within the prison. Holmes too seemed to notice the lack of any activity caused by our commotion.

"That is curious," he uttered. "Quick Watson, now is your moment to exhibit your skills as an actor." With the blood racing furiously through my body, my mind was as quick as Holmes'. In the limited time that we had, in that gloomy chamber and in constant pain, I tore down the sheet and draped Holmes with the filthy rags. With his gaunt posture, the formidable London detective looked like one of the many beggars that filled London's busy streets. As for myself, I put on the guard's jacket over my shirt and placed his cap on my head.

Taking the keys from the floor we cautiously emerged from the chamber. Holmes leaned against me as we headed down the corridor and followed the direction the guard had come from. It was a long, dim narrow tunnel. A few small openings high above in the ceiling let slip rays of sun which stopped us from tripping on the rough brickwork beneath our feet.

As best as I could, I attempted to play the part of the prison guard should we encounter any other officials along the way. Holmes, meanwhile, staggered blindly forward clutching at my right arm. His pretence was not so far detached from the truth. Soon we approached our first complication as the path veered towards the left behind a concealed corner. I slowed my pace, holding Sherlock Holmes closer to me. The fear of discovery had momentarily drowned my pain as we turned round and found ourselves facing a locked gate. I fumbled through the keys in my bloodied hands in the hope of finding the right match. Attempting the first one yielded no success for the lock remained secure. Time passed by and the pain had returned to plague me. The second fitted straight through the keyhole but stuck.

At that moment, my heart faltered. Movements could be heard faintly from the ceiling above us. After a few moments of silence, I attempted another key. This time it slid into the hole, twisted round and a dull clang unlocked the gate. Leaving the corridor behind us, we found ourselves in a confined inner courtyard with dark, bare brick walls on all sides, except for a low door with a staircase leading up to a passage on our right and a postern in front of us.

As we crossed towards the centre of the courtyard a few muffled voices broke out from the top of the stairs. Holmes pushed me away from the direction of the sounds, so I made for the other opening. We passed through the old, unguarded postern which led us up a small flight of steps and out of the northwest side of the prison. Having been accustomed to the darkness of the prison cell, the stronger light outside was uncomfortable.

It was early morning and the sun was still in the lower regions of the eastern sky, but its rays hurt my eyes and the throbbing in my head did but intensify. Yet, through the fear of discovery and pursuit, I felt new strength rushing through my body as the pain became numb, although our progress was slower than my friend had anticipated.

My legs were weak and with Holmes clinging tightly to me, still assuming the role of the blind beggar, we limped past the pedestrians, whose curious glances increased my uneasiness. Gradually, we managed to limp our way into the relative obscurity of Giltspur Street and recover our strength. We leaned against the door of an abandoned warehouse, cowering behind a pile of blackened wooden boxes that had once carried piles of coal through the London streets. As we gained some rest, the pain in my back returned. It was exhausting trying to stand up straight and fight off the spasms. Holmes too seemed worse than before. He crouched down and tightened the tattered bed sheet round him. He trembled in the cold morning air. The tranquil safety of that street was but a mockery of the danger that awaited us in the open, as well as the fear of the prison which still stood too close to our hiding place.

Upon Holmes' suggestion I discarded the uniform and, rummaging through the refuse around us, I utilised the remains of a black coat to cover myself and placed a trampled bowler hat on my head.

"A proper factory worker no doubt," smiled Holmes through his chattering teeth, "but perhaps still recognisable as the dashing Dr Watson."

How he came to the conclusion without the use of his sight was beyond me. Perhaps it was his wish to exert additional caution which made me reach out for one of the empty boxes scattered around. Rubbing my hand against one of the inner sides, I scraped off some mucky residue and proceeded to smear the contents on my forehead and left cheek, before adding a few stains on Holmes. With the theatrical preparations now over, we rested once more behind the pile of boxes, concealing ourselves from the watchful eyes of any passersby, expecting the inevitable alarm to be raised at our disappearance.

As the sun rose higher, I could examine the state of my friend's eyesight. The redness of the gash across his face was more pronounced. The skin around the eyes was tender and dotted with small blisters as a result of the fire. I resisted trying to clean the wound itself, fearing it might lead to an infection. I therefore bound his eyes with the cleanest rag I could find, to protect them from any further damage until I had the opportunity of a better inspection.

"We must go Holmes, I fear we have tarried too long," I whispered, looking at a factory worker who passed us by with a suspicious glance.

"Right again Doctor. But we cannot hope to go to 221B before first investigating further. No doubt our imprisonment has been known only to a handful of individuals in league with our stalker. Whoever brought us to Newgate did so without the knowledge of Scotland Yard or the prison officials themselves.

"The silence Watson. The silence which reigned around our chamber is not a common occurrence at Newgate. I believe our enemy had secured a confined area of the prison through his powerful friends and set a personal guard to watch over us before we were smuggled to the gallows at the noon summons today. We are therefore in no obligation to hide, for in the eyes of the Law we are innocent men, but for the sake of precaution and in the hopes of providing an exciting adventure for your writings, we shall wade unseen from inquisitive eyes through the streets of London."

Holmes smiled and raised his left hand against my shoulder in order to stand up. I assisted him as best I could before we headed out into the bustle which spread along Holborn.

"You shall be my guide Watson. You know my methods. Observe everything, rule out nothing!"

It was a strenuous journey. Our attire was not welcomed by the cab drivers we accosted along the road. We were therefore forced to walk on foot, step by step towards Holmes' intended destination. It was his express purpose to survey the scene of the explosion from the other night. We therefore made our way towards Gower Street, leaning on each other and halting every now and then. I had no clear indication of which route we were taking, but I followed my friend's directions as he named the streets through which we were meant to travel. Suffice to say, it took us more than an hour before I finally glimpsed the green patch of trees as we approached the familiar quarter of Bedford Square Gardens from the northwestern end. We had made our way through Oxford Street before turning round into Rathbone Place and finally veering back south towards Tottenham Court Road.

Before leaving Oxford Street, we had stopped by a telegram office after Holmes instructed me to send a note to Mycroft with the following message:

The baker seeks fire in the yard.
Two by two one by 6.

The message was ambiguous and without meaning. Had I not complete confidence in my friend's capabilities, I would have thought these were the ravings of a madman. Having done as requested, we followed the rest of the route. It was past twelve o'clock and, by the time we crossed into the Gardens, we were exhausted but Holmes was eager to press on.

We eventually found a tranquil resting place close to the outer railings, away from prying eyes. A few passersby strolled casually in and out of the Square, but kept a safe distance from the area of the explosion. Through the hedge I was able to look over across the street towards the ruined building. A dark, smoking pile of wreckage stained the corner where the printing house once stood. Broken pieces of brick and timber, burnt paper and mounds of ash were scattered around the area. A few men laboured in an attempt to gather the debris and clear up the street. The scraping noises of spades and exchange of loud voices, as the workers shouted instructions at each other from various points, rose harshly in the still air.

"Watson, what do you see? Every detail, every nuance," whispered Holmes with some urgency. His hands trembled with suppressed excitement as he crouched beside me. I described the scene as best I could until my eyes fell on the building itself. The wall where the door had once stood had been knocked down. Only a few feeble brick frames remained to prevent the structure from collapsing completely. I looked more intently at a figure walking amid the wisps of white smoke that still emerged from the heaps of rubble inside.

The pain in my back had worsened, but I drove the discomfort out of my head and peered further through the bushes, intent on laying my eyes on the individual prowling within. Pushing away the low-hanging branch of an elm tree from before my eyes, I climbed onto the low stone wall supporting the railings and looked across. From the ruins, out into the street, there emerged a tall man with a grim stare, brushing some ashes off his army uniform.

A cold chill ran down my spine. The unmistakable and imposing figure of General Kenward, whom we had had the misfortune to encounter in one of our cases, coughed and cursed whilst looking at the wreckage around him. I identified the man to my expectant friend who smiled in acknowledgement.

"Well, at least we know who our stalker's powerful friends are," remarked Holmes quietly.

"You don't think the General ..."

"How naïve Doctor! Of course I do. Was it not his declared intention, despite my brother's assurances, to retaliate after being humiliated during the Trafalgar Square murder case?"

General Kenward paced up and down the pavement with an expression that would freeze one's blood. The workers outside avoided his stare and instead hastened on with their task. A second man then came up behind him; a familiar face with a distinctive visage. He was young, tall and slim while his attire conveyed the characteristics of a gentleman. His behaviour, as he emerged from the ruins, was in stark contrast to the General.

Calm, quiet and exhibiting a unique keenness in his glance, he wore a long black frock coat over a pair of equally black trousers. The collar of his white shirt reached up under his clean-shaven jaw whilst a top hat sat upon his head. From where I was hiding, his attitude and appearance reminded me of someone from the recent past, but I was unable to properly assign a name to that man. He came out with his hands behind his back, carrying an umbrella. I described all of these details to a silent Holmes, who was displaying a perceivable fervour.

The agitated General turned to face the newcomer and they shook hands whilst his voice was heard far above the workers' scraping spades. It was nonetheless hard to make out what was being said, but the destruction of the printing house and the loss of much of its contents was the main cause that threw General Kenward into a rage.

This altercation went on for a few minutes, during which the other man remained silent. As the General's arguments died down, the younger man smiled, a peaceful smile riddled with sarcasm which did not go unnoticed by the other, who shook a finger threateningly in his face before turning abruptly and heading for a nearby hansom. As the cab thundered away, the young man's smile brought to my mind a sudden recollection, the reason for which I did not at first understand, of a bank in Charing Cross Road. After a moment he turned away towards the demolished building, with his hands still cupped behind his back, holding the umbrella.

I looked down, dwelling on the thought that had occurred to me. Fragments of conversation and visions played in my head, until I finally recognised that kindly face.

"Michael Scrawley," said Holmes suddenly. His tone of voice seemed distant and weak. He sat motionless, resting against the railings. Like a vicious stab at my heart, I remembered the name and his association with us.

Looking back across the street, there was no doubt that the man was indeed Michael Scrawley. The young banker from Cox & Co., who had greeted us so courteously during our investigations into Richard Stanbury's death, was at the heart of this tangled web. I felt sick at that realisation and the pain in my back intensified as I thought how such a man, so eager to assist us in that case, could turn out to be the stranger who had stalked our every move and brought us so close to death.

Holmes had clearly come to the same conclusion before I ever did. Back at the prison he said he had narrowed down the possibilities, and my description of his appearance and attitude towards the General seemed to indicate the banker as the only remaining possibility.

My companion rose painfully to his feet.

"We must go Watson, haste is required." His voice was low but an urgency lay hidden within it. Intent on discovering more, I ignored his summons and kept my eyes on the man who had caused us so much mischief. He had paused a while beside a large mound of debris on the corner of Gower Street, looking towards the British Museum. He seemed wrapped in thought until a young boy came running towards him from the direction of Bloomsbury Street.

The boy stopped in front of him and presented a piece of paper before running off. The moment the man set his eyes on the contents, he turned round and shouted at one of the labourers who had been busy shovelling the debris back into the building. The banker's sudden turn of character was remarkable and frightening. The way he gestured and strode forward in his wrath was beyond belief.

"It seems news of our escape has reached him at last. The thought of both our necks free from a noose must surely be agonising for him," Holmes smiled grimly, for it was Michael Scrawley's turn now to raise his voice above the calm atmosphere of the surrounding streets.

"We must leave Watson, now for it!" My friend pulled me back from the fence, where I had a last glimpse of our stalker climbing into a carriage. As I stepped down from the stony base, a sharp pain ran down my right leg. I lost balance and slipped, clutching at the tree branch in an attempt to prevent a fall. My grip was weak and I tumbled back onto the hard wet ground, pulling Holmes down with me.

The impact on my injured back was too much of a strain. I roared in agony and twisted round to my side as the tender muscles pulsated fiercely. My mind wavered once again between consciousness and numbness as the pain drove out all sense of reason and comprehension. I felt I had been on the ground for hours before someone seized me by the arms and pulled me up onto my knees. The pain was still overwhelming but my mind slowly regained its mastery.

It was then that Holmes' voice reached my ears.

"Steady Watson!" he whispered, but his words sounded harsh and loud. He dragged me to my feet, but I staggered forward once again into his grasp. I found it difficult to breathe as I leaned on Holmes. The fall and sudden spasm had made me nauseous and unsteady; I was chilled and my entire body shook relentlessly. Regaining some strength, I looked upon Holmes' helpless frame and recalling our plight, gripped my friend's arm and dragged him out of the square.

As we limped across the street into Tottenham Court Road, a carriage drove past us. Looking up, I beheld the features of Michael Scrawley looking in our direction. By the look in his eyes, it was evident that he had recognised his former captives. Feeling a rising terror at being discovered, I hurriedly pulled Holmes towards the other side of the street. He seemed to realise what was happening and quickened his pace alongside mine.

I did not look back, but I could hear the hooves behind as the hansom swerved and turned towards us. We plunged forward into Percy Street, and concealed ourselves behind an overturned cart by the side of the road. Still in agony, I lay crouched and motionless, with my arms over Holmes' head. Not daring to look out from our concealment, we heard the distinct screech of a carriage being drawn abruptly to a halt and a clatter of footsteps rushing past us. The commotion soon died down but we did not dare leave our hiding place for some time.

As Holmes rightly suggested, we could not go straight to 221B. The sun was still too high and our escape would surely draw unwanted attention towards Baker Street. We had to lie and wait for the evening to aid us before we attempted to return to the safety of our lodgings. We therefore embarked upon another slow and arduous journey towards Marylebone, where we stopped at a small inn in Chiltern Street. There we waited for the sun to dip behind the surrounding brick houses before heading cautiously out into the cold just after half past five.

During that time, still desperately clinging to my right shoulder, Holmes was entirely under my protection and guidance. One false step on my part would have proven disastrous and our exploits around this mystery would have dissipated into thin air. I took as much care as I could, hastening past the lamp-lit areas to find refuge in the shadows. Eventually, the familiar façade of 221B was in sight and by that time, the pain in my back had become unbearable. My head throbbed mercilessly and I could hardly move my legs, but for Holmes' sake I was determined not to fail him at the last minute.

As we shut the cold outside, the warm and secure sitting-room of 221B raised my spirits. Mrs Hudson was nowhere to be seen. I placed an exhausted Holmes into his armchair by the mantlepiece and began peeling off the bandage to inspect his wounds. It took me a few minutes to disinfect and clean any residue from his eyes, in order to prevent any further harm.

His wounds would take a few days to heal and fortunately there appeared to be no permanent damage to his eyes. Gently, he managed to open his left eye, but still found it difficult to see clearly. Upon Holmes' insistence, I only covered the right eye with a fresh bandage, leaving the other exposed for my friend to be able to attend to a few simple tasks until his sight returned to normal.

Tired out and having performed my duties as a doctor to the best of my capabilities, I fell onto the sofa without thinking about the persistent back pain, but my bones ached with exhaustion.

"Thank you Watson," came the soft voice of Holmes from across the room. There was an unusual gentleness in his tone of voice and the gratitude never felt as genuine as at that moment.

We both lay there for some time in the silence of the room, without a care for our pressing dangers. Eventually a door was closed shut and the voice of Mrs Hudson could be heard echoing downstairs. This was followed by a heavy set of footsteps ascending the staircase.

"Mycroft, is that you?" I heard Holmes utter.

"You did say six, didn't you?" enquired Mycroft Holmes, as his heavy frame strode into the sitting-room.

"I see you've successfully deciphered the contents of my telegram then," said my friend, tilting his head slightly to look at his sibling standing before him.

"Rudimentary," answered the older brother.

Sherlock Holmes laughed at my bewildered expression, the first sign that his eyesight was making a steady recovery.

"You see Watson, that illogical note I had you send was a simple cipher in case the telegram fell into inquisitive hands. 'The baker seeks fire in the yard' is my rather whimsical way to indicate some present danger and the request of Scotland Yard's officials. 'Two by two one by 6' is purely transparent and an indication of our meeting place here at six o'clock.

More footsteps were soon heard coming up the stairs and there appeared the figures of Gregson and Lestrade, who almost collided in order to be the first to reach the sitting-room door.

"Good heavens Holmes!" exclaimed Lestrade, seeing my friend lying in his armchair with his wounds.

"Merely a slight impediment Inspector, nothing more. Nonetheless, your concern for my wellbeing is appreciated," smiled Holmes. "Kindly sit down."

With our guests seated, Holmes explained with his usual preciseness of details, all the critical points of interest that led up to our unlawful incarceration. Mycroft was visibly flustered at the revelation of General Keyword's devious side. Perhaps he was more confused by his failure to spot that crooked character than anything else. The Scotland Yard inspectors looked confused by the amount of information, but maintained stern expressions and nodded at every statement.

"The game is afoot gentlemen, it is time to act." Holmes leaned forward in his armchair as he began to outline the next stage of the investigation.

Throughout my friend's statement, I lay motionless on the sofa, having found the most comfortable and painless position to rest in. I dreaded the inevitable, when I would have to stand back up to take my leave. As I felt a wave of exhaustion coming over me I struggled to follow the conversation which ensued over the next hour or so between Holmes and our visitors. In the end, forcing myself, I rose from the soothing resting place and bid goodbye to those present.

With many an appreciative remark and a few warnings of caution from my friend, I staggered out of the room.

Leaving the warm comfort of 221B, I made my way furtively back to my own house and a no doubt anxious Mary; all the while as a shadow seemed to follow my every step.

The Bloomsbury Scandal

From the outset, I must impress upon the reader that the following account will differ stylistically from the usual writings of Dr Watson's stories in *The Strand*. The good Doctor himself, recovering from his recent predicament, has asked me to bring this cycle of cases to a definitive conclusion.

"It is your story. You must write it yourself," he said to me weakly. Therefore, I have made it my task to present the reader with those facts that have led to the conclusion of this most singular affair, which had begun to haunt us over the previous months.

It was that time of year which is particularly relished by most people around the world, being the festive season.

December 1888 was in the grip of a fierce winter that threatened to force London to a complete standstill. My mind, impervious to the physical afflictions assaulting the human body during this season, was replete with shadowy visions of Michael Scrawley. Our first encounter at the Cox & Co. bank invaded my thoughts: every detail, every nuance of his behaviour critically dissected in the hope of yielding results. Without further investigation and fresh data, however, I could not pursue the matter any further. With Watson earning his long-due rest, following our unlawful incarceration, I lay in my lodgings recovering from the injuries I had sustained. My eyesight was rapidly returning to normal, but my process of observation was temporarily muddled by a hazy screen, which transformed the joy of analysing details and intricacies into a cumbersome task.

To occupy my time, I took the opportunity to indulge in a case or two which were so simplistic in nature, that the resolution of each was attained by the mere account of the client and a quick draw from my pipe.

Yet, the lethargy of the human body is fatal to the aggressive mind.

Thankfully, one morning before this staleness threatened to turn to madness, Lestrade burst into the sitting-room short of breath and agitated.

"What is it Inspector?" I asked, whilst going through the day's newspapers scattered on the carpet.

"Murder, Mr Holmes," replied the Scotland Yard official amid his panting.

"Glorious! Care to elaborate?" I rose to my feet, feeling the idleness beginning to dissipate, but caught the sudden hesitation in the inspector's demeanour.

"Well, it's …," he began. "It's General Kenward, he was found dead early this morning."

Like a sudden flash of lightning, the case of our stalker became simultaneously so delightfully complex and simplistic. Without a word to the expectant inspector, I went into my room to put on my coat.

With due caution and apprehension, I ventured out of 221B and emerged onto the snow-caked pavement of Baker Street, before climbing into the cab that awaited us.

On our journey I sensed a distinct change within the London streets. Passersby seemed wary when strolling amongst fellow pedestrians. The bustle of commuters, which always rose harshly in the morning air, was dull as if hushed by the recent news of the explosion in Gower Street, sending justified fear into every heart of this city's inhabitants. Or perhaps it was the brewing rumour of a looming war. Whatever it was, London, mirroring my own state of mind, held its breath before an approaching storm.

The murder had occurred in Rutland Gate, Knightsbridge, a street adorned with impressive terraced houses. One of these was the General's own home, which lay on the north side overlooking Hyde Park. I followed a nervous Lestrade up the main steps of the house, stopping on the doorstep at the entrance. There lay the body of General Ambrose Kenward, attired in his military uniform, slumped against the front door with one hand still clinging to the brass knob, and his legs splayed out on the icy stone steps. The once grim and arrogant face had been replaced with one of intense agony and horror. The cause of this predicament and presumably his death, lay in a wound on the right thigh which appeared through a tear in his trousers.

Upon closer inspection, it was evident that a chemical of sorts had been somehow injected into his leg. The lens I brought before my eyes magnified the subtle details and hidden clues. The small incision in his leg showed that the chemical had reacted with the skin and had resulted in a large red rash of blisters and creased skin. I took a sample from the wound to examine it further, along with a few drops of the orange-coloured liquid spattered in and around the wound, and out of which emanated an acrid smell. An acidic compound had clearly been the cause of such severe damage to the skin tissue and the fabric of the trousers, and had resulted in complete cardiac failure. His death removed any loose ends, allowing me to focus my investigations directly on Michael Scrawley.

A quick glance at the interior of the house, with its lavish corridors and exquisite rooms, yielded no further clues and I furnished the inspector with as much information as I allowed myself to reveal.

"Has the storm finally arrived?" he asked solemnly.

"It has," I replied, turning my back on the house.

Before returning to Baker Street I dispatched a telegram to my brother Mycroft requesting information.

There were two primary lines of inquiry I wished to pursue at that point. Although the identity of our stalker and his poisonous methods had been revealed, there was the disconnected thread of Scrawley's association with John Openshaw from *The Five Orange Pips*, and his influence on a number of our cases.

With these thoughts occupying my mind, I arrived at 221B and headed straight to the kitchen for an analysis of the sample I had brought with me.

Only a few experiments were necessary before concluding the cause of the General's demise: aqua regia, a combination of nitric and hydrochloric acid, used to dissolve specific kinds of metals. It is mainly used in the restoration of artefacts, but is a toxic substance once it comes into contact with the skin or injected directly into the bloodstream. Deadly, unless treated within minutes of exposure via thorough cleansing of the wound. General Kenward had been caught off guard and alone, unable to seek the necessary help before he succumbed to the poison.

With this new revelation in hand, I headed for my bedroom – that retreat which had been concealed for so long from Dr Watson himself. There, upon the walls and the floor lay a structural map I had been constructing over the past months: a tangible fragment of thoughts and ideas on my current investigations into these latest cases, an interconnected series of newspaper cuttings, notes and telegrams establishing an entire chain of reasoning and theories. On the carpeted floor at the centre of the room, around which the entire map revolved, lay a small piece of paper with a question mark on it and the name 'Michael Scrawley' written beneath.

His young, concerned face at our first meeting haunted me. What his ultimate purpose was, and how he would achieve it, was at the heart of this riddle. Following the General's death, there was to be no more prowling in the streets in search of evidence. The conclusion to this prolonged case lay in that room. I had to discover the truth once and for all.

Sitting upon the bed, with a bag of tobacco beside me and my trusted clay pipe to hand, I sat motionless and explored the deep recesses of my mind, unearthing the details and hypotheses I had created up to that point.

I analysed all the events and facts in order: Michael Scrawley learns about the death of John Openshaw and begins his destructive retaliation against me and Dr Watson. He meddles in some of the cases and brings us into close contact with Death at several instances. He works in the shadows, occupying a senior position at the Cox and Co. bank, upon Charing Cross, as well as owning a private printing house in

Gower Street. Poison is his preferred method of delivering the fatal blow. He provides Mrs Stanbury with naphtalene, before she herself meets a similar toxic fate. Dimethylmercury, which laces the letter I received in November, is a rare toxin that is hard to come by. Not to mention aqua regia, the acidic substance that has caused the General's death. Where in London could a young man gain access to such a wide variety of poisons? Surely not? Yes, yes. The connection is there. Only specialised individuals could have access to such substances.

As the mist slowly cleared before me, my eyes fell upon the name 'Hugh Ashmore' scribbled on a piece of paper. Dr Ashmore, the medical professional employed at St Thomas' Hospital, had disappeared suddenly with his entire family, leaving behind him a disconcerted governess, an empty house and the fragments of an envelope bearing the same floral and angelic insignia from the printing house. Could this have been the result of a strained relationship with Michael Scrawley? Perhaps the latter had requested Dr Ashmore's assistance in procuring the toxins. A request the other had refused and thus was forced into hiding from such a dangerous man.

Yes, that had to be the salient point.

At that moment, there came a knock on the front door of the lodging. Although irritated by the intrusion, I could not let pass any potential information.

I was greeted by a young man who handed me a telegram, took the small coin I offered him and left. Walking back towards my bedroom I read the contents:

Openshaw and Scrawley. Maternal half-brothers.

— Mycroft

The lock was broken and the truth began to materialise. This explained the ferocity with which our stalker had so eagerly sought revenge against us. A few more draws on my pipe led me into a frenzied investigation of the source from which Scrawley acquired the poisons. There were numerous ways in which these could be obtained through obscure negotiations with delinquents. Yet, they could not all be accessed from a single, specific location. I needed to narrow my search to institutions, scientific buildings, anything that could justify the presence of naphtalene, dimethylmercury and aqua regia all together in one place.

I hurried across the room and pulled out a large map of London upon which I had scribbled several notes on streets and buildings to outline my adventures with Watson during our cases: Streatham Street, Vicarage Gate, Trafalgar Square — all laid out like a chronological story reaching its culmination at an unspecified destination.

Puffing furiously at the pipe, bellowing plumes of smoke that enveloped the entire room in a milky haze, I marked down all potential targets. An urgent mood grew in me, the instinct of the detective perceiving some approaching doom and the ticking of the clock. Every minute lost was another step closer towards an unforeseen tragedy.

My finger traced all possible locations: the Royal Society, the Natural History Museum, the British Museum. My hand hesitated over that historic landmark. Its close proximity to Scrawley's printing house in Gower Street was too much of a coincidence. Surely the museum's conservation department had access to such deadly chemicals for more scientific reasons than to deal death to fellow human beings. As these thoughts raced through my mind, I glanced at a piece of crumpled paper which had been saved from the explosion Watson and I had been caught up in. Its edge had been singed but the words printed on it were legible:

Grand Unveiling of Sir George Whittock's
Armoury Collection
British Museum

At the bottom, almost indistinguishable, was the same insignia from the printing house. The chain of thought had been fashioned, the link was complete.

Michael Scrawley, whose primary occupation was that of a banker, also earned money through his printing house, assisting the British Museum in promoting its available knowledge to the scientific community and the general public alike. The ironies of life were truly a delicate thread. No doubt Scrawley's charisma and amiable nature granted him some liberty in exploring the Museum's less public quarters in search of his chemicals.

As I had just concluded that one final piece of investigation, I put on my coat when all of a sudden there came another knock at the door, louder this time and with much more urgency. Expecting another telegram boy, I was perplexed to find Mary Watson on the doorstep. As her husband had remarked in *The Sign of Four*, the young woman was striking in appearance for her composure and simplicity. Her eyes, a well of concern and agitation, looked up at me in earnest. It was a common trait I had detected on many occasions in clients seeking assistance to their pressing problems.

Mystified by her presence there, I took a step backwards in silence and allowed her in. She entered, clutching both her hands, as she glanced nervously around her.

"Mr Holmes," she cried. "He's gone, they've got him!" Her voice quivered in trepidation.

She took a step closer, extended a trembling hand and held out a crumpled note. I took the paper and read its contents:

Seek Sherlock Holmes. Doctor Watson lies waiting.
The time has come.

A sudden, incomprehensible dread overwhelmed me. We had come to the uttermost end of the mystery. The stage was set. Watson's peril was a trap to lure me to a final confrontation. I looked at Mary's expectant expression, tears running down her face. I had little to go on, and my brief search through the possible locations had not been properly substantiated. Against everything that I hold so crucial in the quest for Truth, I took a risk. I trusted my instinct, for Watson's sake. I stretched out a hand to the tearful woman in an attempt to comfort her distress, despite the cloud of despair that had settled on my own heart.

Taking leave of Mary, I raced downstairs and took a cab to the British Museum.

As I made my way to Bloomsbury, past the frosty window

panes and streets blanketed in white, clouds loomed overhead. It was a dreary journey, and interminable. Thoughts of John Watson, powerless in peril, and the vindictive character of Michael Scrawley, grinning in his triumph, plagued me. I knew not whether I was heading to the right place and, if I was, what terrible fate awaited there.

Emotions clouded my judgement, and reason was replaced by doubt.

It was past two o'clock when the cab came to a sudden halt in Great Russell Street as pedestrians were seeking shelter from a cold drizzle that had just started. The towering exterior of the museum loomed in front of me, with its colossal pediment and soaring columns in veneration of an illustrious Ancient Greece. The construction itself embodied the pinnacle of human feat in architecture and knowledge.

Rushing across the South entrance courtyard, I made my way up the soaked stairs and plunged into the building, leaving the cold and persistent rain behind. I was greeted by the soft flow of visitors walking into and out of the front hall. Unsettled and disoriented, I stalked the hallway, seeking for any signs of Watson and his captor. I recalled once more the varied chemicals Scrawley had used for his heinous purposes, and further validated my supposition. It had to be there, somewhere inside the museum, where countless artefacts were processed and restored before put on exhibit. Preservation of precious historical items relied on the use of acids to aid the cleaning process.

Lacking any other clues for evaluation, I raced through the hall and up the main staircase towards the upper levels, intent on taking another risk based on insufficient data by exploring the conservation facility within the museum. Surely, that was the most probable location for the storing and use of uncommon chemicals.

Oblivious to the crowds along the vast and complex system of interconnecting corridors, I hurried past the domed Reading Room and the King's Library, aiming for a little portal by the side of an intersection on the East Wing of the building. Upon arrival, I observed a small plaque on the wall by the entrance:

Conservation Division
Scientific Laboratory and Research

I pushed the door open and entered a dim chamber. It was a small, reclusive area with three windows on the right side. A few streaks of light filtered through, falling on several stools and tabletops replete with an array of intricate vases, paintings and stacks of vellum, all laid out at the centre of the room. There was also an assortment of the finest tools and scientific equipment: test-tubes, burners, pipettes, water basins and specialised utensils. Closing the door behind me and shutting off the noise of the bustle outside, I ventured further in.

Exercising appropriate caution was critical. Although small, the room was high and each step I took echoed threateningly throughout. Adorning the walls were diagrams and charts outlining an array of scientific subjects, from periodic tables to world maps. I glanced to my right, noticing a bulky cabinet placed beside the first window. Its glass-paned doors provided a glimpse of an extensive collection of chemicals stored in vials and jars of various sizes.

"Impressive, wouldn't you say?"

The voice that rang out of the shadows startled me. At the farther end of the room, where the light was dimmest, stood two figures – one tall and erect, the other hunched low with his hands before him.

Stepping forward, the young Michael Scrawley revealed himself. He wore the same dark attire as when we first met at the bank. He leaned on an umbrella, gripping the hooked handle in his right hand. He gave a subtle smile laced with mockery. Behind him stood Watson, his hands tied. A contusion was visible on the left side of his forehead and along with his unkempt hair and dishevelled clothing, it was evident that he had met his capture with fierce resistance. He raised his head and looked with an appreciative nod.

"You are a tenacious man, aren't you Mr Holmes?" sneered Scrawley. "All that inconvenience, all the planning and the loss of my printing house just to be rid of you, and yet here you still are."

"I imagine that all this has to do with John Openshaw," I replied.

My mind recalled that young man's anxious face on that stormy night when he came to seek my comfort and assistance.

"I failed that boy, Scrawley," I confessed, "but I could not avoid the fate he met."

"You betrayed him!" he screamed. His calm countenance morphed into some hunted beast. "You betrayed his trust and loyalty, and sentenced him to a cold, solitary death." He stamped his feet on the floor in protest, before suddenly calming down.

"Poor, poor dear brother. Poor John," he said in a quiet voice to himself. "Well, the time has come."

In one subtle movement, he turned round, raised his umbrella and stabbed at Watson's leg, who collapsed to the floor. He screamed in agony and clutched at his left shin.

"Aqua regia," sneered Scrawley, "but surely you had already guessed." He raised the point of the umbrella and for the first time I could clearly see the distinct glass tip as light glinted off it. Like a deadly syringe, Scrawley had found a way to conceal his lethal methods in the most trivial of objects.

I rushed forward to my friend's aid before stopping short. Watson lay wailing in agony as Scrawley pointed his weapon towards me. He stared viscously in my direction.

"Not to worry, I've left some for you too."

I was unarmed and any false move could prove catastrophic. As we both stood there, facing each other in the dimness of the room, he lunged at me with barbaric agility. The toxic tip drove through the air at my head. I sprang backwards just in time to avoid the fatal thrust. Scrawley instantly took a step forward and came in with a second jab. I took off my hat and flung it at my assailant's face, blocking his view. His renewed attack was foiled, and he was forced to lower his umbrella to deflect the hat.

Seizing his momentary disorientation, I ran forward and drove a clenched fist against the lower part of his jaw. He cried out in pain and staggered backwards, but his strong physique enabled him to steady himself firmly. Without pausing to consider his next move, I pressed on with the attack and extended my right leg behind his left knee to block his movement, turning my back on him. Applying a sharp elbow punch to his stomach, I concluded with a firm grasp of his right wrist and twisted it round, forcing him to drop the weapon before tightening my leg further and causing him to lose balance and fall to the floor.

At that moment, Watson's agonising moans echoed throughout the room. I looked up and abandoned the grasp on my opponent in order to rush to his aid. Before taking another step, I was held by the left leg, and toppled over to the floor. Turning round, Scrawley's frame loomed over me as his powerful punches came fast and hard on my chest and abdomen. They were driven with trained precision and considerable energy. The unceasing force of the blows left me out of breath, but my attacker was also left in want of air. His powerful offensive had tired him and, as he got to his feet, he looked around for his umbrella.

My breathing was strained and my muscles ached. Watson's moans reached my ears. I forced myself up but was instantly brought down on my knees by the sheer pain that spread across my body. Scrawley was already lunging forward with a renewed attack. This time, he swung his umbrella from below his waist to bring it back up and skewer me through the chest as I was staggering to my feet.

He was almost on me. Still on my knees, I quickly slipped my left arm out of my sleeve. In one swift motion, with my right hand, I swung the coat round, just in time to catch the umbrella's tip and parry off the stab. I twisted my arms and tightened the coat around the weapon to secure it. I had momentarily halted the attack, but restricted eyesight prevented me from detecting the swift, serpentine manoeuvres of my opponent. Scrawley shifted his hold on the umbrella, using the handle to lock my right arm and twist it out of use. As bone and muscle were stretched beyond their limit, the pain became sickening and a numbness swept through my shoulder and fingers. I lost my grasp on the coat as Scrawley abandoned his grip on the umbrella and slammed his right palm against my bruised chest, again and again until he pushed me back, slamming me to the ground.

My head hit the hard, smooth floor. Fighting off the sudden dizziness, I looked over to the left. The hazy vision gradually cleared, revealing Watson's body lying feebly against a bench.

"Watson!" I cried in a weak voice, as the strenuous contraction and expansion of my lungs held me down. My companion, whom I had so unjustly involved in this peril and failed to protect, had fallen silent. Immovable.

At that moment, a shadow loomed over me. Looking up, there towered Scrawley once more, brandishing his weapon. Despite his painful breathing, a savage sneer crossed his face. The deadly spear suddenly came into view, ready to thrust its toxic contents into my body.

Readying for his final act, he raised the umbrella high above him, before using all his force to plunge it down into me. I closed my eyes, expecting at any moment the sharp glass tip to pierce my flesh.

The lethal point struck and a shattering sound rose in the

air. Several fragments flew into my face. I opened my eyes to find the umbrella on the floor beside me with pieces of glass scattered all over. The honey-hued aqua regia fluid had drained out and now lay staining the decorative tiles. Watson's hand clung to Michael Scrawley's shoulder, before he was pushed to the ground where he lay motionless.

Aware of the sudden interruption and seeing my opponent bereft of his deadly weapon, I utilised the hesitation to mount one last attack and bring this criminal to justice. I rose and lunged forward and caught his right hand under my left arm, whilst placing my right leg behind his left, using the palm of my free hand to ram it repeatedly against his jaw and tilt the head backwards. My retaliation was less effective than intended. The aching bones and muscles in my chest and arm prevented me from delivering a successful blow to knock out my foe. Instead, my attempts only served to hold off Scrawley's counterattack and increase his wrath. In response, he grabbed my wrist with his left hand and twisted it round. Injured by his previous attack, my arm succumbed to his movement before he broke free and went for my neck.

His grip was firm and decisive, depriving my brain of oxygen. We were locked in a tense duel of strength, him with his right hand on my throat and me with my other arm firmly clutching his left elbow. As I felt the blood rising to my head, I looked into his glaring eyes. In that critical moment, it struck me how clear and young they were, full of promise and determined resolve. They reminded me of Watson's own keen glance whenever we set out on one of our cases, and how he constantly looked towards me with undeserved admiration during my deductions; it was his friendly gaze that had become an important part of my life during the last few years.

However, these thoughts dissipated and, once again, I saw before me Michael Scrawley's ferocious expression as he tightened his hold.

A feeling I had rarely experienced before, a mixture of pity and rage, coursed through my body. The sudden fear of death gave me new strength, enough to punch him with my numb fist and push him away, before catching hold of him from behind by his coat collar and applying a conclusive kick to his left knee. Pulling as hard as I could, I flung him down to the ground onto his back, knocking him unconscious. Reaching for my coat nearby, I rolled him over and pinioned his arms mercilessly behind his back, preventing him from breaking free unless he desired to dislocate both his shoulders in the attempt.

Without a second glance at my fallen enemy, I staggered forward towards Watson. His face had gone pale. Sweat had formed on his forehead and an acrid smell rose from the ugly stain on his left trouser leg. Tearing off the fabric revealed a scarlet stain on his shin. The skin around it was wrinkled and the wound had started to fester, as the acid penetrated deeper inside the sinewy tissue. Time was running out. The damage would worsen if untreated and there was the strong possibility of the toxin infecting his blood irreversibly.

Heedless of my own pain, I raised him up and dragged him across the chamber towards one of the basins filled with water. I rummaged through the many tools and utensils, gathering several tubes and pieces of fabric lying on a table. Laying Watson against one of the benches, I pumped water from the basin through the tubes to wash the acid from the wound. It was a long and arduous process which required a constant and careful administration of fresh water to make sure none of the acid remained. With my bruised arm, I struggled to open up the wound for cleansing, and after several attempts and constant washing, there was a visible change in the colour of the skin around the lesion. I bound his leg with some cloth and proceeded to open one of the nearby windows. The cold December air rushed in and drove away any remaining fumes emanating from the acid.

Exhausted, I sat beside Watson making sure his breathing was constant. The keen air which blew inside, mingled with the scent of rain, was refreshing. After a few minutes, my companion stirred and sighed as colour returned gradually to his face.

"Holmes," he said weakly, "thank you." He held out his hand and patted me on my arm.

It impressed me in a way I never thought it could. The simple gratitude he extended in his predicament gladdened my heart. At that moment, seeing Watson's half-shut eyes staring back up at me, removed the shadow of fear which had lingered so persistently during those months of strife, more so than ever on that day of despair.

"Help me, Watson," I said. "Never allow me to forget these trials. They are a reminder of my imperfections and occasional inability to safeguard my clients." My mind recalled the dreadful events that had brought John Openshaw to 221B.

However, before running the risk of delving too much into the emotional, I shall abandon any further writing, and conclude the matter swiftly. Michael Scrawley was arrested in connection with the murder of General Kenward and the abduction of Doctor Watson. Furthermore, his other criminal involvements were exposed and he was brought to trial, after which he soon found himself standing on the wind-swept gallows at Newgate prison.

The good Doctor himself recovered. Slowly at first, for the acid had caused severe damage to his already weak leg, but his strong will and the affectionate care of his wife soon had him back up on his feet.

With the case successfully concluded, I retired to 221B and once again was privy to the wailing and pleas of clients who sought comfort and assistance in their plights. Stalking anew the streets of London in pursuit of hidden clues and buried secrets was the medicine I needed to recover from my trials.

It is therefore here that the matter rests.

It was with a sense of surprise and relief that I read Holmes' account of his struggles against our unstoppable adversary. Once more, it is time for me to pick up the final threads of this account. Holmes claimed the limits of the case had been reached, but I shall add this brief epilogue to it.

The repercussions on London's administrative status were severe. General Kenward's criminal involvement posed a strain on the government's efficiency and reliability in the eyes of the public. For an individual to have occupied a high-ranking position, and then be involved in such a conspiracy, was damaging. Not to mention the shocking revelation that such a promising and successful young man as Michael Scrawley could turn towards the devious side of the criminal world and commit such heinous acts. Nevertheless, as with many things, progress heals most wounds and England's reputation endured, albeit this scandal persisted as an unpleasant scar in the annals of its history.

My own physical scar remained for a long time. The wound still pained me and gave much discomfort but, with the help of Mary and the knowledge that this long-winded mystery was finally concluded, my mind rested all the more easily.

The bond with Sherlock Holmes became stronger and he always found me eager to assist him in any of his new cases. I also noticed a distinct change in his character. He appeared to be more empathic, more thoughtful, more human. The first signs of this manifested themselves a few days after the Scandal, and I was on my steady way to recovery. Mary and I received a summons from my friend inviting us to spend Christmas lunch with him at 221B.

It was quite an unexpected surprise but the offer was gladly accepted, and on the day we headed for Baker Street, to my companion's lodgings. Sherlock Holmes greeted us with an unusual warmth as he came forward and shook my hand in earnest. He smiled and looked at me with that same keen glance I had seen many a time, except it was significantly more welcoming and compassionate.

"Merry Christmas, Watson," he said. He looked at my wife and bowed, before heading back towards the mantlepiece to pick up the violin and play the most exquisite carol I had yet heard him perform.

Also from MX Publishing

MX Publishing is the world's largest specialist Sherlock Holmes publisher, with over a hundred titles and fifty authors creating the latest in Sherlock Holmes fiction and non-fiction.

From traditional short stories and novels to travel guides and quiz books, MX Publishing cater for all Holmes fans.

The collection includes leading titles such as *Benedict Cumberbatch In Transition* and *The Norwood Author* which won the 2011 Howlett Award (Sherlock Holmes Book of the Year).

MX Publishing also has one of the largest communities of Holmes fans on Facebook with regular contributions from dozens of authors.

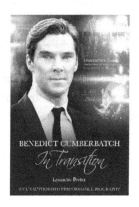

www.mxpublishing.com

Also from MX Publishing

The Missing Authors Series

Sherlock Holmes and The Adventure of The Grinning Cat
Sherlock Holmes and The Nautilus Adventure
Sherlock Holmes and The Round Table Adventure

"Joseph Svec, III is brilliant in entwining two endearing and enduring classics of literature, blending the factual with the fantastical; the playful with the pensive; and the mischievous with the mysterious. We shall, all of us young and old, benefit with a cup of tea, a tranquil afternoon, and a copy of Sherlock Holmes, The Adventure of the Grinning Cat."
Amador County Holmes Hounds Sherlockian Society

www.mxpublishing.com

Also from MX Publishing

The American Literati Series

 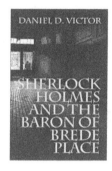 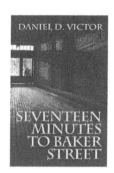

The Final Page of Baker Street
The Baron of Brede Place
Seventeen Minutes To Baker Street

"The really amazing thing about this book is the author's ability to call up the 'essence' of both the Baker Street 'digs' of Holmes and Watson as well as that of the 'mean streets' of Marlowe's Los Angeles. Although none of the action takes place in either place, Holmes and Watson share a sense of camaraderie and self-confidence in facing threats and problems that also pervades many of the later tales in the Canon. Following their conversations and banter is a return to Edwardian England and its certainties and hope for the future. This is definitely the world before The Great War."
Philip K Jones

www.mxpublishing.com

Lightning Source UK Ltd.
Milton Keynes UK
UKHW02f0940150118
316165UK00011B/612/P